Captivated

by

Kathryn C. Kelly

Cover designed by Crystal Cuffley
Published by Makin Groceries Media
Rosenberg, TX 77471

Kathryn C. Kelly
Visit my website at www.katkelwriter.com

Printed in the United States of America

First Printing: Aug 2018

ISBN-13 978-1-7-73889-3-6
Library of Congress Control Number: 2018955411

ACKNOWLEDGMENTS

Thank you, Crystal Cuffley, for your amazing work and amazing support. Friends, fans, and family, this wouldn't be possible without you. I have to give a special shout-out to Danni List Werner. You have yet to jump on a jet and strangle me for always changing the text AFTER you'd corrected chapters. Vincent Luckett, we miss you so much and wish you lived closer. Hearing about home helps me to keep things in perspective. Melanie Cooper, you rock! Angie Stanton, we have to have another pizza date. Emma James, thank you for being a sounding board even in the midst of writing your amazing Hell's Bastard Series. Melissa Kulis, you are awesome! Memaw/Fluffy/Mama/Memaw Kelly, you are an amazing woman. You always help me see the light at the end of the tunnel and inspire me to continue on. You're my hero. I love you and I will always be here for you. Katie, Alegra, and Zoey, my beautiful babies, you are the wind beneath my wings. My girls, you challenge me, you encourage me, you amuse me, and you amaze me. It is my privilege and pleasure to have you as my daughters. It's always said it takes a village to raise a child. It takes a village to publish a book. Without all the aforementioned people in my life, this wouldn't be possible.

DEDICATION

Melissa Kulis, thank you for all your wonderful work.
You're the best!

CHAPTER ONE

*T*here wasn't much in life Dominic Luca sought to accomplish and failed to achieve. Now, he had to find a way to murder Blaine Bradford without penalty.

Pacing in his hotel room, Dominic paused in front of the window, glancing down at the shadows of palm trees and buildings at the foot of Canal Street. Dusk's colorful skies had graduated into an indigo night.

He conceded Bradford was above-average, but the asshole had more luck than sense. Either that or he'd been tipped off to Dominic's discovering his crime. *Where the hell is Bradford?* He wished he knew. It would save him time and frustration, but so far, neither he nor his men had been able to track Bradford down.

The sonofabitch had hacked into Dominic's proprietary files, the ones with his negotiations and detailed plans to expand his corporation. If not for one small mistake Bradford had made as he'd spoofed Domamill's system during the subsequent theft of company files, Bradford would've gotten away with the hacking. Thank God for that error. Dominic cringed, thinking of the havoc that would've been wreaked if things had gone smoothly for Bradford. No one would've been the wiser until Bradford produced Dominic's expansion plans, financial data, targeted companies to acquire, and company data. Instead of Dominic being a silent partner in Bradford Industries to save it from sinking, Blaine could've used the data for capital gain and sank Dominic's firm, too.

He gritted his teeth and gripped the windowsill, sincerely wishing he was squeezing Bradford's neck. Part of the reason Dominic had come to New Orleans was to go over company policy with Bradford, now that Dominic had bought into the asshole's corporation. Dominic had been in the car, halfway to the meeting, when the head of his IT department had called him with the news. The fucking ingrate. Dominic had already invested a lot of money to turn the man's company around, even agreeing to keep Blaine as CEO and president. Though the takeover hadn't been hostile, it hadn't been completely mutual either.

A knock on Dominic's door tore his attention away from the streetcar barreling down the tracks that divided the lake-bound and river-bound sides of the street. Devising his next move, he went to the door and opened it, revealing Albert, one of his bodyguards.

"We think we've found him, sir," Albert offered, jumping to the heart of the matter. He rarely smiled and preferred being a lone wolf. His taciturnity matched Dominic's.

"I don't pay you to think. I pay you to *know*."

Albert's face and entire bald head reddened, but he offered Dominic a tight-lipped nod.

"Where *might* Bradford be?"

"Not far from here, sir. At a charity auction where his sister is participating. Whoever bids on her gets to take her to lunch or dinner and her bid proceeds go to her chosen charity."

The details of this benefit gala were unimportant to Dominic. This woman's interests held little interest to him. For that matter, *she* didn't matter either as long as he got his hands on Bradford. "Bradford has a *sister*?"

"Apparently, sir."

"Did you find out much about her? Her age? Is she married? Have children? Does she have a connection to Bradford Enterprises?"

"We don't believe so, sir. As far as we know, she isn't married and we're unsure of her age. We didn't have time to gather much information about her. We thought you'd want to know as soon as possible."

So Bradford had a potential weakness. Dominic needed to investigate this further, see firsthand how he could use this woman against her asshole brother. *Perhaps I should attend the event.* "What time does this auction begin?"

"It starts in half an hour, sir." Albert shifted his weight and cleared his throat. "The fact that he has a sister comes as a surprise."

"So it does," Dominic agreed, although if Bradford had behaved, his sister's importance would've been nonexistent. "How does she look?"

Albert flushed. "We aren't sure."

"I'll find out myself. I've attended enough of these fucking events to figure out who's who. "Good work."

"What about his sister, sir?"

She could be useful in getting Bradford to see the error of his ways. Bradford might be an asshole, but even assholes protected their families if a threat arose against them. Not that Dominic intended to hurt the lady. He'd just insinuate it so Bradford complied with Dominic's request to return his files and his money.

Dominic shrugged. "What happens to her depends on her brother's cooperation."

"Yes, sir. We'll keep a tail on her—"

"No need, Albert. I'm going to the event."

"Sir?"

If Dominic wasn't so annoyed, he might have laughed at Albert's shock. Everyone knew charity functions bored him to tears. "Bradford might be there to support this woman, so I'm going to the event. We need to get a move on as soon as possible. I'm calling Scanlan to make sure he has the plane ready for takeoff once we get asshole." Dominic would arrive at the function late. He didn't intend to return to the hotel, so he needed to alert his pilot, pack the little clothing he'd brought with him and settle his tab with the hotel. Meanwhile, he also needed to devise a plan to retrieve Bradford without anyone noticing. Any other intentions Dominic had depended on Bradford's attitude and responses. Yes, Dominic wanted to choke the fuck out of Bradford, but murder wasn't his usual style. If Bradford turned into a special case, then he didn't need anyone seeing him forcing Bradford to go with him.

"Even if Bradford's in attendance, do you think he'll willingly go with you?"

Dominic appreciated Albert's perception. "We'll find a way."

"Sir, I don't know if this is a good idea. There will be a lot of witnesses."

"I don't remember asking your opinion. If there's a chance to find Bradford, I'm taking it. I've been in this goddamn hotel room to lull Bradford into believing I'd backed off." If he would've joined the hunt, Dominic wasn't sure if someone would've alerted Bradford that

Dominic was looking for him, so he'd allowed Howie and Albert to do it. "Wait for me downstairs in the lobby," he said. "Be ready to move when I am. That'll be all for now."

He started to turn away but Albert stopped him.

"We do know her name, sir," he said.

Why did the admission sound so begrudging? "Which is?"

"Olivia."

Offering a brusque nod, Dominic saw Albert out, anticipating the moment he got his hands on Bradford, with this Olivia's help or without.

Where are you?

Pressing the send button on her phone to deliver her text message, Liv rocked back on her feet. She stood one girl away from having bids placed on her for a charity near and dear to her heart. At the moment, though, she wanted to locate her boyfriend in the audience. He'd promised to bid on and win her. It was their three-month anniversary and they planned to make love tonight to celebrate. In anticipation of her deflowering, she'd gotten on birth control three weeks ago.

Liv had more than her ninety days as Garth's girlfriend to rejoice about. Her paid tuition had secured her acceptance to Louisiana State University for the fall semester. She'd taken her first monumental step toward her goal of becoming a pediatric oncologist.

The cherry on the frosting, however, was Garth's promise they'd indulge in hot sex, champagne and chocolate. He'd already given her one lesson on pleasure, making her touch herself while he watched, teasing her to distraction. Her body ached for release from the constant state of arousal she now experienced. So, where was her soon-to-be lover? Tonight, he'd promised they'd go straight for the final exam. Not wanting to appear completely ignorant about positions and technique, she'd given herself Sex Ed 101 by reading erotic blogs, watching a few online porn videos, and purchasing sex manuals, flavored oil, handcuffs, blindfolds and satin ties.

"Ladies and gentlemen, Miss Olivia Bradford." The voice over the loudspeaker blared, startling her from her thoughts. "She practices Zen and Tai Chi. Recently accepted into LSU."

So recent, in fact, Liv hadn't even mentioned it. She scowled, balling her fists. Blaine must have told the committee, making her wonder what else her brother had blabbed about.

The spotlight haloed her and Liv squinted against the bright glare as her eyes adjusted. Regrouping, she glided out of the shadows, determined and proud.

The dim lights concealed the elite of New Orleans, dressed in their finest. Every now and then, someone shifted and a gemstone glittered in the glow from the candlelight. Whispers fluttered through the air and she stood straighter, drawing from the well of tranquility she was learning through Zen.

The master of ceremonies, Mr. Charles, fell silent, because she'd listed only a few accomplishments on her bio. She didn't want to land in jail so she couldn't very well claim hacker and thief on her resume. The other girls from wealthy backgrounds had time to volunteer and earn community hours and go on shopping sprees whenever the urge hit them. They didn't have brothers as crooked as the Tower of Pisa.

The silence stretched Liv's already taut nerves. She scowled at Mr. Charles, wishing he'd encourage a bid.

"May I have an opening bid of one thousand dollars?" he said, acting like a mind reader instead of a jerkwad.

Hostility radiated from the guests like a dangerous nuclear device. Was it because she was Blaine Bradford's sister? No, half-sister, not that *they* knew. They believed he was as wealthy as they were. By extension, they believed Liv to be just like the other rich girls, whose families were power players, entrepreneurs, politicians, entertainers and athletes. No one knew Blaine teetered on the edge of bankruptcy after destroying the Bradford empire with singular focus. He should be grateful to Liv for getting what he needed to save his ass, though Liv knew better.

She thought he'd at least be here. As thanks, he could've attended the event he'd insisted she participate in. Realizing she hadn't seen her brother since the night before last, she frowned.

"One thousand dollars for Miss Bradford, sister of Blaine Bradford, CEO and President of Bradford Industries."

Grumbles. Murmurs. Shuffling. Blaine evoked all those reactions, so Liv related.

Whether or not Blaine—or her boyfriend, Garth— attended, her charity of choice, a local cancer society, was a good one. Someone should open their wallets and cough up the starting bid. A small commotion captured

Liv's attention and she craned her neck to glimpse the identity of the three people filing into the room. Thanks to the crappy lighting demanded for this dinner and auction, she couldn't discern if the newcomers were male or female.

Mr. Charles cleared his throat. "Can I get one thousand dollars for Miss Bradford? Her cause is a good one. Breast cancer research. Anyone can bid. Man or woman. Young or old. The winner gets to escort Miss Bradford to lunch or dinner."

Unlike the fuss from moments before, Mr. Charles statements quieted everyone. Silence reigned. Absolute, deafening silence. Annoyance assailed Liv. Images of the various ways she'd murder Garth rolled through her head. Tai Chi balanced her and aided her serenity but it strengthened her too. She might've practiced both Zen and Tai Chi for only a few weeks but she was sure she could take down Garth.

If Blaine didn't keep himself surrounded with security, she'd murder him as well for putting her in this predicament in the first place. But he had an amazing sense of self-preservation. With Bradford Industries sinking fast, he'd needed another cash infusion, beyond what he'd received from a new business partner. The check Blaine had waved in front of her for her college fees prompted Liv to agree to Blaine's hacking request. Without proof that he could, and would, pay, she would've stayed far away from his illegal activities, instead of spending long hours cracking Domamill Enterprises' system. Finally, after weeks, she got in successfully. The moment she did, Blaine began hovering over her, demanding more files than they'd originally talked about and rushing her to get it done. Of course, she hadn't wanted to linger on the company's system. The longer she'd dallied, the greater the chance for the IT department to pick up on her activity. Not surprisingly, Blaine had refused to listen when she told him the hacking could be traced if she made one small screw-up. In which case, she'd be spending her time in a prison dorm rather than a college one.

Liv was glad the whirlwind of rehearsals and preparations for tonight were over. Gladder still she'd played her cards just so and gotten what she wanted. It hadn't been easy. Not at all. She'd done her time as her brother's maid, cook and computer expert.

Stop sweating, Liv. Everything is going to be fine.

She and Karen, her BFF, planned to go to Hilton Head tomorrow afternoon once Liv and Garth parted company. After almost two years of hell, she could live like a fun, fearless, college freshman. She would be finished working for her asshole brother to repay him for her mom's hospital care. She'd slaved away for him and before Liv realized it, time had flown by and the hours she could've spent working to earn money for college had been used serving Blaine. When she'd gone to him with news she wanted to fill out her college application, he'd sworn to help her with school and promised he'd come up with a reasonable repayment plan. Even now, she cringed at how she'd felt discovering Blaine's true regards toward her. They'd bargained for two entire days. His initial idea had Liv being an escort to some of his business associates. Then he'd suggested she keep his bodyguards entertained.

He'd wanted to turn her into a whore on his behalf. Looking back, she couldn't understand why she'd been so shocked. Clearly, there was no love lost between her and Blaine. If she'd ever doubted it, his suggestions had removed all uncertainty.

Once she pointed out that if anyone discovered Blaine Bradford's sister whored herself out it might reflect badly on him, he'd backed off. Just as they'd reached an impasse, he'd come up with the hacking idea. If she didn't serve some purpose for him, he had no use for her. He would've put her out of his house and left Liv homeless. He was a big dickhead like that.

Remembering her debate over her limited options made her purse her lips. It had been to either accept Blaine's latest job. His even more crazed ideas had ranged from setting her up with a sugar daddy to getting her a job as a stripper. She could've put off school for another year or two and work full-time in another menial job to save what she could. With stripping, she worried about her safety. Foregoing college again ran the risk of life derailing her plans, in which case, she'd never receive her degree. Her mom's intentions for Olivia hadn't included earning money any way she could to eke by like she had.

"This is a cause near and dear to Miss Bradford's heart. Her mother passed away from breast cancer thirteen months ago."

The words caught Liv's attention and she drew in a sharp breath, losing the smile plastered on her face. She blinked hard, her throat hurting with the effort not to break down into sudden sobs. Mr. Charles exploited her mother's death with cool detachment. Not only hadn't she given him permission to reveal such a thing, she hadn't ever mentioned how and when she'd lost her mother.

Blaine. Her face burned and she eyed the gleaming stage floor. Blaine's connections had gotten her on this stage, so of course he felt entitled to blab about her personal life. Asshole.

"A thousand dollars. One is all it takes."

Nothing. Not a peep. She'd never expected such a reaction, otherwise she wouldn't have put herself in the position of being on this stage, even to repay Blaine for his help. If not for her new motto of no regrets and no more running away, she would've wished she'd never turned to Blaine. But Liv had held out hope that with chemo and good doctors, Connie could beat the cancer. In the end, it had only prolonged the misery and made Liv beholden to her brother.

Once her mother died, Liv had considered skipping out on Blaine. He was an asshole and she hadn't placed many boundaries on how she'd repay him. But she was done running. Her mother had kept them moving from one place to the other. As the end drew near, however, Connie had been filled with regrets and Liv didn't want the same for herself. She didn't want to be on her deathbed, wishing she'd made different choices.

Mr. Charles cleared his throat—again. He was a tall, stern man, his reddish-blond hair going gray. He adjusted his horn-rimmed glasses and straightened the papers on his lectern. The glare he directed at her made Liv rock back in her imitation Bettye Mueller heels. She wrestled with her temper, restraining the urge to flip the man off.

Another tedious moment passed before the spotlight moved away and focused on the blonde next to her. Unlike Liv, in her strapless black gown, the other girl sparkled in red sequins and diamond jewelry.

"Ahh, Miss Andrea Wallingford, ladies and gentlemen," Mr. Charles purred. "A true New Orleans jewel."

Liv's phone buzzed and she winced, sure the noise of an incoming text message could be heard right down in the French Quarter.

"Fifty thousand dollars for Miss Bradford." The commanding voice didn't belong to Garth or Blaine. Garth's was a little less cultured and Blaine's much more condescending.

Liv froze, her sharp intake of breath drowned out by the rising voices in the crowded ballroom.

"I beg your pardon, sir?" Mr. Charles sputtered. "What did you just say?"

"Fifty thousand dollars." The man enunciated each word, allowing no room for misinterpretation or refusal. "For Miss Bradford."

None of the other girls had brought in as much for their bids. Liv grinned, pleased to her toes, not caring that a stranger, instead of Garth, had flung out the number.

"Olivia Bradford?" Mr. Charles's skepticism grated. He made it sound as if she wasn't worth fifty thousand dollars. "We've moved on, sir. The opportunity to bid on her came and went a few minutes ago. Would you care to bid on Miss Wallingford?"

"No."

Implacable. The one word gave Liv the impression power and autocracy filled the man. And he wanted her. Tension knotted her stomach and she floundered at the sheer force of his tone.

"Sir—"

"I want Miss Bradford," he echoed, as if he'd read her mind.

He made the statement sound lurid and sexual.

"You want Miss Bradford for fifty thousand dollars?"

"For however much it takes," he murmured in a silky baritone.

Her curiosity jolted her and Liv took a step forward, wanting to see this man.

"Miss Bradford, please remain in place."

She halted at Mr. Charles's abrupt chastisement but her whole being filled with expectation and anticipation. Like a lover waiting to open a Valentine's gift, she wanted to know this man's identity.

The spotlights on the track above the stage flickered on, illuminating the area below the stage and bouncing off the silver candelabras, the pristine white tablecloths, the rims of the gold-plated serving dishes.

Bathed in the bright light, the man was breathtaking. His blue eyes focused on her. His appraisal burned with intensity, roaming over her body. His interest unnerved her. The air felt ignited with their mutual awareness. Golden blond hair lay askew on his head as if he'd just rolled out of some woman's bed. His angular face showcased a straight nose, a square jawline, a firm chin and a set of beautiful lips, the bottom one fuller than the top. He captivated her, held her spellbound and she flushed, heat rushing through her. Wide shoulders filled the dark-blue suit jacket while the matching trousers encased his long legs. A light-blue tie, double-knotted, ringed his strong neck. He exuded danger and arrogance, reminded Liv of a marauding berserker and her senses bounced around in a wild rush. Their gazes clashed and his nostrils flared. He seemed as if he wanted to eat her up and spit her out. She searched her mind for a memory of him. She sensed she knew him. Or should know him. He repeated his inventory of her body, lingering on her breasts then traveling to her waist and legs, undressing her with his eyes. Liv resisted the urge to shield her body with her hands, conscious of his virility and sexual magnetism, her clothes inadequate protection against his pillaging perusal.

He smirked at her then turned a cool focus on Mr. Charles. The bidder lifted a blond brow, a silent command to commence with the bidding.

"Er, fifty thousand dollars for Miss Bradford. Can I get sixty thousand?"

Liv glared at Mr. Charles's back, wishing she had the capability to incinerate him. He knew he couldn't get sixty thousand dollars for her. She'd stood up there for three minutes before the blond–haired stranger had sauntered in.

Another text message alert dragged her attention away from the man to look at the screen. She smiled upon seeing Garth's name. Awareness of the other man remained, however, and her fingers shook as she held the phone up to read.

I know what you did. A frown creased her brow and she wondered if the message was a joke. Was he trying to spook her because he remembered how frightened she'd been when they'd watched that old horror movie last week? No, that was *I Know What You Did Last Summer.*

I know who you are.

She shook her head, the first text more meaningful with the second one added. He knew her identity and her hacking crimes.

No! No! No! He couldn't know.

Think, Liv. Think! She snapped her attention to the stranger, his sudden appearance taking on a whole new meaning. The man might be law enforcement.

Insane. Law enforcement wouldn't place a bid on her. They'd storm the place and drag her offstage in cuffs. She gazed at the tall blond man again. Amusement danced in his eyes. He enjoyed her panic, which she knew was plain on her face by the violent throbbing inside her that indicated the extent of her fear.

Who was he? She and Garth had been a couple for three months...would he have sent the authorities after her?

Liv shook her head in denial, falling back on her original assumption that she would've been dragged off the stage in an undignified manner, not get a fifty thousand dollar bid and become the envy of every girl there.

She'd been so careful, so protective of her unstable childhood with the frequent moves and the days when she and her mother had nothing to eat. Garth knew that? He knew she was the daughter of a woman who had done whatever she needed to provide for Liv? No. That couldn't be. She'd hidden that even from Blaine.

Her mother's choices had rarely been right but, most of the time, they had been noble. She was her mother's daughter, though, doing what she thought necessary to provide care in the remaining months of her mother's life and what was necessary to get into college.

Garth couldn't know that either.

Perhaps Garth knew she wasn't wealthy, just Blaine's bastard half-sister.

He'd not believe Liv belonged here amongst the elite and the wealthy, wearing an imitation designer gown, tight shoes and cubic zirconia.

"Going once!"

She was fifth in the lineup and more preening girls needed auctioning off. Beads of perspiration broke out all over her body. She'd have to get through the rest of the bidding and then go make nice with the man who'd won her. She'd have to smile and set a date for their meal.

"Going twice!"

Garth's sister was on the stage and the event was a huge highlight of the social season. Blaine had insisted she take part, apparently thinking that by having her up on this stage, he'd somehow prove to society what a loving big brother he was, showing off his little sister. What a load of garbage! Liv had agreed to participate because *she* wanted to show everyone she might be "just Liv" but she was as good as they were. She wanted to show Blaine that, in spite of how far beneath him he insisted she was, she deserved to be treated as a Bradford.

"Sold to the gentleman standing in front of the stage!"

Sold to a stranger. Not Garth, the kind of boyfriend most women dreamed of having, whom she'd believed had a heart and, unlike her snake-in-the-grass brother, cared about her.

"Miss Bradford, please come with me," the gorgeous guy ordered.

"That's impossible, sir!" Mr. Charles said. His deep voice should've been pleasant instead of being the most annoying sound she'd ever heard. "The girls cannot leave the stage until the auction is completed."

"She leaves now to arrange our date or I withdraw my bid," came the annoyed response.

Liv wondered how many others knew whatever Garth had found out. People were shifting in their seats—chairs sliding, utensils and crystal clanking. The impatience in the room was growing like an ominous thundercloud.

"I'll leave," Liv blurted. She'd make her departure before one of these people rose and pointed a finger at her.

"I'm sorry but—" Mr. Charles paused at his wife's approach.

The event director, Mrs. Charles, rushed onto the stage, holding a clipboard in her manicured hand. She tugged her husband away from the microphone and whispered in his ear. Whatever his wife told him, the man's eyes widened and he nodded, his hawk-like features abashed. He clutched the wooden sides of the lectern and nodded at Liv.

"Miss Bradford, you may leave."

Now that the moment of truth had arrived, apprehension rooted Liv to the spot, a chill chasing down her spine. Goose bumps rose on her skin, screaming at her to run the other way. The berserker's inscrutable blue gaze focused on her, lingering on the swell of her breasts before traveling down the length of her body.

His hair reminded her of corn silk and she wanted to run her fingers through it and repair the disorder.

He moved and Liv remembered her uncertain predicament. Her brain wasn't functioning. Cast under his spell, she'd agreed to go with this man.

He could be one of her brother's enemies. The thought careened through her and Liv gripped her phone, her mouth going wood-chip dry. *Ridiculous again, Liv.* Blaine's enemies wouldn't bid on her.

She only needed to go and set a date for their lunch or dinner. The internal melodrama was unnecessary. Although she'd run with her mother time and again, now that Connie was dead, Liv wouldn't run anymore ever again. From anything. She had nowhere to run now, anyway. Not to Garth. And Karen, the closest friend Liv had ever had in her life? Not to her either. She couldn't pull Karen into this.

Both Karen and Garth hailed from the country-club set and were family members of two of Blaine's business associates. God. Blaine. He'd told her no one could ever know her mother had been their father's maid. He was going to kill her.

"Miss Bradford, exit the stage *now.*"

Turning on her heels, she clutched her phone and hurried to the steps on the side of the stage. Two men in suits similar to her bidder's met her at the bottom, crowding her in. Both were muscular and tall, one bald and the other sporting short hair. A moment later, the berserker was placing his hand at the small of her back and leading her out of the ballroom into the nearly deserted receiving hall, the two other men following. His touch burned through Liv's simple dress and she wished she'd worn more than a thong and pasties beneath. Though he didn't know she was all but naked under her gown, she did, and she felt bare and exposed, vulnerable to the man's unknown intentions.

Outwardly, she remained calm, but her heart was racing. She couldn't figure out who these men were and what they could possibly want with her. Despite how they intimidated her, she tried to convince herself they were harmless. They wouldn't expose themselves if they weren't.

Besides, the man who'd won a date with her looked and sounded too refined to be dangerous.

Her awareness of him made her nervous. He sidled a glance at her and tingles coursed through her, settling deep in her belly. And she remembered how the evening had been meant to go. In Garth's bed and in his arms. Her bag!

"Wait," she said. She placed her hand on the man's arm, finding no give, only rigid muscle. Once they made their arrangement, she'd call for a cab to get home then contact and confront Garth about those text messages. "I need to collect my things."

A muscle pulsed in his jaw. "It's been taken care of."

His voice slid through her and her core throbbed. She breathed in the spice of his cologne and the scent went straight to her head.

"Please," she whispered, reluctant to remove her hand from his arm. He was tall, sculpted, and golden. The epitome of masculine perfection. Mystery and intrigue surrounded him but she couldn't deny how drawn to him she felt. He differed from Garth as much as the sun differed from the moon. Garth was rangy and lean with manicured hands and hair combed just so. Unlike her current escort. While this man's nails were neat and groomed, his hands didn't look soft and pampered. And his hair. Her fingers itched to touch those beautiful, messy golden locks. Reining in her wayward thoughts, she leaned closer to him, so aware of him her nipples ached and her belly clenched. She should be appalled at her response to him. Only an hour ago, she'd considered herself in a relationship with Garth...who'd abandoned her. The latest in a long line. As she'd been forced to do through bitter experience, she set her face to the future. "You don't know which table I was sitting at. I need my bag."

"I have it." His teeth flashed white against his golden skin and amusement glittered in his eyes. "Yours is the black bag filled with intimate items. Shall I name them?"

A gasp accompanied her acute embarrassment and she narrowed her eyes at him, the way his mouth moved when he spoke making her wonder how his lips would feel against hers. Her phone vibrated again, alerting her to another text message, this one from Karen.

Garth is saying the strangest things about you.

Liv cringed at her friend's message. Karen knew nothing about Liv's past so her friend would have a thousand questions, would want to extract every small detail. Having someone else confirm what Garth now knew increased Liv's suspicions she'd been outed everywhere. She flushed, all her reasoning about Garth and accepting life as it came to her pounding through her head. The hurt and unease blocking her logic had no place in her life. Both would cause her to hesitate in her choices for whatever arose next. Worse, she'd also *regret* and second-guess her decisions.

Connie's last words to her had been, "I'm so sorry, Livvie."

Sorry for what, Liv didn't know. Moments later, her mom had slipped away, leaving Liv to assume she'd meant the way they'd lived since Connie had described in detail all the things in her life she'd do differently if given the chance. Even when Liv had reassured Connie that she'd lived her life the best she could, working with what she had, Connie hadn't been appeased. Liv believed her mother loved her but sometimes Connie had said things that sounded as if she'd regretted having a child.

Her attention divided between Karen's text and her escort's last question, Liv stumbled but the blond man's quick reflexes saved her from falling to the ground. His big hands lingered at her waist, his long fingers flexing against her. His hand at the small of her back set a spark to her blood. In silence, he guided her to the area set up for payments.

As he halted, the other two men stood watch, silent guard dogs. Who was this man? Unable to deny her sense of dread, she peeked toward the door and the two men closed in around her.

A quartet of white-haired society doyennes, dripping with diamonds and reeking of money, sat at the table. Should she mention her alarm to them? If she was wrong about the danger she picked up on, she'd make a fool of herself and her blond berserker would cancel his bid.

"May I help you, sir?"

The brisk sound of the woman's voice made Liv realize she was questioning herself. She'd decided to walk off the stage and go with the man, so she'd stand by that choice.

He held out the slip of paper with all the necessary bid information. "Yes, ma'am."

Liv?

She scowled at Karen's persistence and punched in her response. *What is he saying?*

"Your generosity is much appreciated." The woman's smile plastered to her mouth, the grimness of it removing any sincerity from her next words. "I'm sure Miss Bradford's charity will be ever so grateful she managed to bring in so much."

The man turned a wry look to Liv. "All for a good cause, ma'am." He handed the other woman his Amex Black, which she processed immediately.

The phone pulsed again and Liv cursed under her breath. Instead of Karen, it was Garth. Anger rushed through her at the names he called her. *Liar* was bad enough, *imposter* even worse. But it was the other names she hated, the profane labels he attached to her. He wasn't accusing her of criminal activity. He was talking about Liv's mother and childhood.

She swallowed, clicking off her phone, refusing to acknowledge her hurt that Garth wasn't giving her a chance to explain. Stiffening her spine, she anticipated her arrival home. One fact she'd make clear when she called and blasted Garth was how little she needed him. Needing anyone put her at a disadvantage. She'd needed Blaine and he'd used it to his benefit. She'd needed her mother and she'd lost her too soon.

Tranquility and serenity be damned. She'd allow no one to get away with saying the things Garth texted. Her promising evening had morphed into a disaster. Before she processed the thought, she was led outside. The awning shielded Liv's view of the night sky while the crape myrtle on the neutral ground and the oleander bushes along the perimeter of the premises ruffled in the hot air.

Noticing her phone, the man snatched it from her and deposited it into his suit pocket.

"Give me my phone," she demanded, her rising anger toward Garth pushing through in her tone.

"No."

She attempted to shove her hand into his coat and grab her phone but he gripped her wrists. His hold wasn't painful but it was strong. The warmth of his fingers heated her skin. Electricity shot along her nerve endings. Awareness of him be damned! He was attempting to intimidate her.

If not for his two lurking goons, she would've acted on the fleeting thought to knee him in the groin. "I thought we were making arrangements for our date."

"We are," he murmured.

The movement of his lips drew her attention. He gentled his hold and Liv's tension eased.

"We can do it tomorrow," she suggested.

"No. Now," he said. "I can always return you and request a refund. Say you reneged."

She narrowed her eyes at him, disliking this second threat to reverse his bid. All she wished to do tonight was confront Garth and then grieve for her mother. At times, she still felt the excruciating pain of her mother's loss, even after over a year. Tomorrow, she'd awaken and box away what she couldn't face and then focus on her trip to Hilton Head with Karen. Liv would create a scenario to feed to her friend, hopefully one that answered any and all of Karen's questions.

"Come," her bidder insisted.

"As if I have a choice," she snapped.

A half smile tipped his mouth. Liv registered the dimples in his square jaw when he smiled. He placed his hand at the small of her back again and urged her forward, the other two men flanking them.

"Who are you, anyway?"

Of course he didn't respond. Instead he ushered her to a black Escalade parked in the fire lane. One of his men opened the door and then the three of them ringed her, their proximity purposely threatening. Though close to ten at night, heat hung in the June air. Beyond the iron and stone fence, cars whizzed by. A fire station was located opposite the auditorium. All Liv had to do was escape and make it across Basin Street on a busy Sunday night.

"I'm not getting in there with you. I don't wish to end up on the news after tiny little pieces of me are found spread all over New Orleans."

"Get. In."

The thought that either Garth or Blaine had sent this man after her persisted. Maybe she clung to the idea to soothe away the gut feeling that going with him was the height of bad judgment. He'd taken her phone. What person who didn't have nefarious deeds on their minds stole a girl's phone?

A danger alert clicked in her brain and she swallowed, opening her mouth to scream.

"I wouldn't do that if I were you," he warned in a steely voice.

"You don't want to do this."

He smirked at her. "And what might 'this' be?"

Uncertain, Liv raised her hands, palms up, and shrugged. "I don't know but—"

"Get in," he repeated.

Though her heart sank, she complied, consoling herself that she was outnumbered *and* her imagination ran wild with insane ideas of kidnapping and murder.

"Okay," she uttered, deciding to capitulate for the moment while she arranged defense techniques in her head. She was too new to Tai Chi to have learned much, other than to practice slow, concise moves. Sometimes she still went too fast. Once she became more advanced, she could remain calm out of habit not practice. As of yet, she hadn't had enough training not to allow some fear and panic to set in.

The blond man climbed in next to her, crowding her, his presence overwhelming and all consuming.

His bald-headed bodyguard flung in her black bag and it jingled, one half of a handcuff dangling out. The door slammed and threw her bidder into shadow. Liv's every nerve ending was aware of him because she was both terrified and attracted to someone she'd just met. The bodyguards climbed in the middle row seats and murmured something to the driver. The SUV rocked into motion.

"If Garth sent you, I can explain everything." His silence unnerved her, a reaction she swore he exulted in. She drew in a deep breath, gritting her teeth against appeasing him. She crossed her legs, glad for the darkness. As long as her voice remained controlled, he wouldn't detect her unease. "Did Blaine?"

Resentment wafted from him. Every few feet, the glare of the streetlights flooded the interior, allowing her flickering glimpses of his angry features.

Liv slid closer to the door. "Who are you?"

"Dominic Luca," he announced as if the name held meaning to her.

Liv knew it should. She'd heard it before. She sifted through her fear to place the name. No such luck. At the moment, images of her body floating in the Mississippi ruled her. "And?"

"And you better pray your brother loves you more than he loves the money he stole from me. He has three days to repay me or else."

Liv didn't like the 'or else' at all, even if Mr. Luca's words didn't make sense. Blaine received money from a lot of people, many of them loans he had no intentions of repaying. "You're intending to use me as bait for Blaine?"

Mr. Luca nodded.

"But you just *bought* me."

"Easier method than grabbing you off the street. You walked away with me to fulfill your charitable obligation. I expect a full refund from Bradford."

"In other words, you're kidnapping me?" she squeaked.

"Bright girl."

Liv turned away and stared out of the tinted window. Not so bright if she'd gotten herself kidnapped. Sheer will made her cling to calmness. Should she make a run for it? Could she? They weren't expecting her to jump out of the vehicle. They might try to kill her anyway, so she'd lose nothing in an escape attempt.

The driver turned from Basin Street onto Claiborne Avenue and Liv knew there were several stoplights along the route. Even if the driver turned on Esplanade Avenue and drove all the way to Wisner Boulevard, there were a lot of stoplights, giving her plenty of opportunities to jump out of the SUV. At the intersection of Esplanade, the red light halted them, her first chance to escape.

The moment Liv placed her hand on the door handle Mr. Luca seized her arm and dragged her closer to him, enveloping her in his hold. She dragged in a breath, trying to control her panic and her reaction to being in his embrace.

Dominic Luca must not know her brother very well if he thought Blaine had a shred of compassion. He'd been born into wealth and felt as if the world should bow down at his feet.

She might as well tell Mr. Luca the truth so he could get on with whatever justice he intended. She clasped her hands together, her nails digging into the back of each. "He's not going to pay."

"Excuse me?"

"He isn't going to pay you to save me," she snapped with impatience, attempting to wiggle away. With very little strain, he kept her in place. In his arms. Close to his body. "Just save me the torture of imagining my death and you the hope of getting your money and do away with me now."

"Since he won't pay up for your safe return, I might just do that."

"Mr. Luca—" Liv gulped then snapped her mouth closed, the name clicking into place.

Dominic Luca.

Two days ago, once she'd gotten the last file Blaine insisted he needed, Liv had seen the name *Dominic Luca* on one of the documents. She cleared her throat. "Dominic Luca of Domamill Enterprises?"

"One and the same."

Fuckity-fuck.

Before she descended into full-blown panic, Liv realized the vehicle had stopped and the doors opened.

Mr. Luca stepped out then pulled her behind him. A plane sat on a runway, the engines roaring, no doubt awaiting her kidnapper. And her. Outlines of other airplanes and hangars told Liv they were at New Orleans Lakefront Airport. A salty breeze from Lake Pontchartrain swirled around them and Liv shivered.

She gripped his wrist. "Don't do this. I'm not important enough to Blaine to spend money to save me."

He ignored her, signaling to the bodyguards and propelling her toward the jet.

She was being kidnapped. Instead of sending the police after them for hijacking his proprietary information, Dominic Luca sought personal retribution. Whatever money he kept referring to, she had no idea. Her only comfort was his apparent ignorance of her involvement. She sincerely believed it saved her from a worse fate and for that she was grateful.

CHAPTER TWO

*D*ominic studied Olivia Bradford, who sat ramrod straight in the tan leather seat across from him. In the living area of his plane, an action sequence from a movie hummed in the air. His bodyguards sat near the guest bathroom and the cockpit, pretending to watch whatever they'd popped into the DVD. They looked bored, a far cry from the buzz in Dominic's veins.

Olivia was a beauty, all long legs, slim curves and delicious breasts. Her black hair sported a simple twist, wisps of it surrounding her oval-shaped face. Thick, sooty lashes framed bright-green eyes, her arched brows accentuating her flawless ivory complexion. Teardrop earrings hung from the tender lobes of her ears, a matching bracelet on the delicate circle of her left wrist. Her black evening gown clung to her and he wondered what was beneath it. From what he could tell, nothing.

His attention roamed to her bag and he listed the contents in his head: handcuffs, satin ties, blindfolds, edible body oil, dildos.

My, my, what a naughty girl he'd borrowed until her brother returned the money Dominic had invested in Bradford Enterprises. The things Dominic could do to Olivia Bradford using her toys. His erection pushed against his zipper and he adjusted his position. Her gaze fell to his groin and she flushed, chewing on her lower lip, drawing Dominic's attention. He imagined nibbling on it, suckling on it before worshipping her nipples and clit.

By sheer luck he'd walked in while she was up for bid. At first, nothing mattered except she was Bradford's sister. Then he'd focused on her, instead of just seeing a woman who shared his enemy's DNA. He'd noticed her hand curled around something, betraying her nerves. It wasn't until a few minutes later, when he'd gotten closer, that he'd realized she held a phone.

He'd felt a twinge of an unidentifiable emotion at the vulnerability he'd detected beneath her bravado. She'd grinned and bared the humiliation of not receiving a single bid. The fact she'd completely disregarded propriety and kept the volume turned up on her phone had amused him, as well.

She'd looked so innocent and sweet, and it had shocked him no one had bid for her. Despite the obvious snub, she'd stood proud and defiant.

Captivated by her and unable to find Bradford, Dominic had made the quick decision to take her in her brother's stead. Once her belongings were identified and collected, he'd intended to make a minimum bid. As he'd walked toward the stage, however, he'd heard the snickers about Blaine parading his sister about, believing her beauty would lull everyone to forget his actions. Whatever the man's actions were, Dominic didn't know, but if they were anything like what Blaine had done to him...

Discovering Olivia's charity of choice, he had increased his bid. The substantial amount had nothing to do with her, he'd insisted to himself

Sitting across from him now, she kept glancing in his direction. Wariness shone in her glade-green eyes. He supposed she was frightened but he wasn't in the business of killing innocent young women because they had slime for brothers. However, until he was certain of her role, he'd afford her the same treatment he would've offered Blaine.

No, not the same.

If he'd had her brother, the man would already be beaten to a bloody pulp. He needed to employ a different strategy with Olivia.

Be certain, a voice warned him.

Every time he considered Bradford's duplicity, Dominic wanted to tear Blaine a new one and spill buckets of the man's blood. Just on general principle, since Blaine was a stupid snot. First, though, Dominic needed his invested money and his company's confidential files returned. The man had no wife, no children, no mistress. Only her, Olivia Bradford, his little sister to use as incentive to facilitate the matter.

Dominic leaned forward, resting his elbows on his thighs, attempting to contain his rage. That he found her gorgeous infuriated him all the more. Currently, he didn't do normal relationships and he didn't show mercy to his enemies. Businesswise, he was his father's son and he took pride in that fact. He was close to erupting, to grabbing Olivia Bradford and shaking her until she told him the truth or kissing her until she begged him to fuck her. Either scenario would work to lessen the frustration, anger and lust riding him hard. Looking at her now, his decision to kidnap her satisfied him.

He knew her type. Society girls. He'd been weaned on them, groomed to choose some rich man's daughter, worthy of the Luca name. Love wasn't required. Money, appearances and connections were. His greatest revenge on Bradford would be sending his little sister home pregnant and abandoned.

Fuck. Could he be that heartless to an innocent woman and his own child? His parents may not have shown him much warmth but they'd never abandoned him. Not like that, anyway.

Besides, today's standards were different. Out-of-wedlock pregnancies didn't carry the stigma they had decades ago. Yet, in *their* world, she'd be damaged goods for sons like him, who were tasked with carrying on the family name. Scions didn't raise other men's bastards.

When he glanced at her, he found her watching him and the urge to reassure her that she'd be fine made him grit his teeth. Instead of acting on the impulse to reach out and touch her, Dominic bumped his knees against hers and she scooted away. The back of her seat greeted her, leaving her nowhere to escape him.

He reached inside his jacket and got her cell phone then held it out to her. Without hesitation, she snatched it from him, their fingers brushing. His entire body tightened at the feel of her soft skin against his. The screen on her cell flared to life, dragging his thoughts away from the magnetic pull he felt toward her. He lifted a brow, aware of the rise and fall of her breasts, the delicate column of her throat.

"I don't remember telling you to turn on your phone."

Her eyelids lowered and she gazed at him through the fringes of her lashes. Lewd thoughts swirled through his head at the sultriness of her expression. "I don't remember asking you if I could turn it on."

A sniff punctuated her words, amusing him, but he covered it with a scowl, needing her so afraid of him, her fear would almost reach out and touch her brother when she talked to him. No man worth his salt would leave his little sister to suffer on his behalf.

A series of vibrations buzzed from her phone. She glanced at it before dropping it onto her lap, which served to draw Dominic's attention to her smooth knees and slender calves, revealed by the center slit in her gown. Her thighs were clamped together, not allowing Dominic one glimpse of the treasure between.

She stared at the phone, the tip of her nose reddening. Dominic wondered what she'd read to upset her so. He'd check later. At that moment, he intended to test Olivia's honesty versus his belief that no man was so spineless he'd leave his sister to fend for herself.

Dominic slid a hand along Olivia's knee, gliding his fingers upward along her thigh. His touch raised goose bumps on her flesh. A bit of fear flashed on her face before curiosity brimmed in those expressive eyes. Desire flushed her cheeks and parted her lips. Her study of him was like a physical touch and he drew in a deep breath, restraining himself from skimming his hand farther until he settled over the pulse point between her legs.

Pressure tightened his balls and his engorged cock became uncomfortable. Standing helped. Her gaze fell to his tented pants and straining zipper and she flinched. He bared his teeth, an animalistic urge to possess her rising within him. She looked too inviting to resist, the signals she sent him igniting his lust. The thought of all the things in her bag added to the fire inside him.

Idly, he wondered if she was as easy as Blaine was criminally inclined.

The thought made Dominic jerk her to her feet. The bodyguards glanced in his direction then turned their attention back toward the television. Dominic dragged her through the sitting room to his bedroom, where he slammed the door and watched as she processed what she believed he intended. She took in the dark silk comforter, already turned down to reveal complementary sheets, and the bed with a slatted headboard and footboard.

Dominic knew the exact moment her thoughts mirrored his and roamed to the handcuffs in her bag. Handcuffs to restrain her for pleasure not captivity. He held her, her breasts rising and falling with her nervous pants. The realization she *had* been kidnapped seemed to settle into her and she wiggled against his hold.

Dominic grabbed her wrists, felt their fragility, stared into her green eyes.

And saw sudden stars when her knee connected with his groin. He released her and dropped like a stone to the floor, the contents of his stomach churning. He couldn't think beyond the pain, couldn't form a coherent sentence. Or a howl. Or a curse. His pride felt as bruised as his cock. Tears leaked onto his cheeks and he swore his junk would never be right again. A moan erupted from him.

Through the haze of humiliation and agony, the battle going on outside the bedroom swirled to Dominic from a distance, demanding he move. Screams for help. Hysterical female. Grunts. Curses. Breaking glass. Flesh connecting with flesh. A slamming door. As the pain receded, he realized he lay in a fetal position. He dragged himself to his hands and knees. His balls were throbbing. Any sympathy he felt for her melted away. She was a Bradford all right, underhanded and deceitful. She'd lured him with her beauty then struck.

She'd attempted to ruin a part of him more precious than any other place on his body. He wanted to charge like a raging beast. He could barely tiptoe. Opening the door, he grabbed the edge of the sofa in the small sitting room of his bedroom, pausing while his insides settled back into place. After her kick, he wondered if his cock still worked.

He glowered. Perhaps he'd use her as a test subject.

More in control of his pain, Dominic continued into the main cabin toward his bodyguards. Broken glass he identified as once being decanters of expensive alcohol littered the floor. The roof and walls dripped with gin and bourbon, the smell overwhelming. Albert, bald-headed, taciturn and quiet, sported a black eye, and Howie a bloody lip.

"Where is she?" Dominic snarled.

Albert's chest rose and fell in rapid pants. "The bathroom." The words slid past lips tightened with anger.

Dominic understood. Not many people bested the bodyguard.

"See to your injuries," he instructed, heading to the small guest bathroom. He found the door locked, just as expected. "Open the door."

"As soon as I get reception, I'm calling the police and I'm not coming out until they escort me away and you to jail."

Instead of answering, he went to the pilot and instructed him to contact air traffic control at Sugar Land Regional.

"Tell them we've had a change in schedule and we're going to Charleston."

"Yes, sir. But we will have to make a stop somewhere to fuel. We're getting low."

"Fine." Dominic turned and headed back to the door. The useless fucking knob locked and unlocked from the inside.

They were low on fuel so he needed to get her and this situation under control. He'd try to reason with her one last time. "Open the fucking door, Olivia."

"Go to hell."

Dominic gritted his teeth, his anger simmering. He slammed his palm against the door. Pain stung his hand and careened down his arm. "Albert!" he yelled, though the man sat not too far away, an ice pack on his eye.

The bodyguard placed the ice on a nearby table and rushed to Dominic. "Yes, sir?"

"Shoot the lock off the door."

Not hesitating, Albert unclipped his 9mm and moved forward with a satisfied grunt. He trained the gun on the lock.

Dominic raised a hand, halting the man. "If you don't want to be shot, Miss Bradford, either clear the goddamn door or open it."

"You wouldn't dare!"

He clenched his jaw at the challenge in her voice and nodded to Albert, giving him the go ahead to fire. He prayed the little fool moved. Albert aimed, squeezing the trigger in three rapid motions. The gunfire resounded like cannon shots in the small space. Olivia screamed as the handle plinked to the floor.

"Tell Scanlan not to worry," Dominic instructed, referring to his pilot. He yanked open the door.

She stood in her bare feet, her complexion colorless. Considering the chaos she'd caused, her terror should've been satisfying as hell but her vulnerability stole some of his satisfaction. She gripped the edges of the sink, displacing her phone and sending it to the floor.

Not giving her a chance to recover and take aim at any of his body parts, he scooped her into his arms. Sweat beaded her brow, though she felt as cold as a corpse. He met her look and it seemed to snap her out of her terror. Adrenaline pumped into her and a wild light brightened her eyes. He could almost hear the drums of war—the call to action—blaring in her head. Before she inflicted any damage on him, he readjusted her and threw her over his shoulder, pinning her legs to him. She pounded on his back with her fists and he slapped her ass, her squeal of outrage making him laugh. Reaching the bedroom, he tossed her onto the bed then subdued her with his body. He trapped her arms above her head, rearing back just before she clamped her teeth onto his jaw.

Fuck, but these Bradfords were goddamn trouble. If he really intended her harm, her actions would've brought it about in spades. What the fuck had she expected to accomplish, fighting him thirty thousand feet in the air with not a friend around?

He lay beside her, keeping her body subdued with his leg and her arms trapped with a hand. He grabbed the V of her neckline with his other hand and rent her gown in two. Pasties covered her nipples, tan against the blue veins running just beneath her skin. Her pussy hair was quite visible to him through her sheer thong.

"If I let you go, promise you aren't going to fight me."

Her gaze shot daggers at him and he knew the moment he released her, she would begin to fight all over again. He had to subdue her. Curling his fingers around the thin waistband of her thong, he yanked.

And finally, finally, she stilled, speaking, her words too low for Dominic to bother with at the moment. He took the opportunity to remove her ruined dress and tie her hands together with her panties, still warm from her body. The scent of her pussy filled his head and he drew in a deep breath. He was going to fucking geld Blaine Bradford for this torture.

Ignoring the sight of Olivia's nude body and the heaviness of his erection, he removed his tie and wrapped it around her feet. The plane was starting its descent and he couldn't trust her not to do something reckless. He hurried to her bag and brought it back to his bedroom, ignoring the sly looks of his bodyguards, a loud thud catching his attention. He ran toward the sound. Just as he'd suspected, Olivia hadn't remained still. She must've twisted in an attempt to free herself and had landed on the floor.

The plane was gliding to a stop. He knew it and Olivia knew it, too. She opened her mouth and let out a piercing scream. Dominic tossed her bag on the bed, lifted her and threw her next to it, knocking the wind out of her. He used one of the blindfolds to cover her mouth and enclosed one of her wrists in the handcuff before locking it to the bedpost. Spreading her legs, he secured one ankle to the foot post with one of her silk ties then did the same to the other ankle. Her legs were close enough to allow mobility and open enough to allow access to her pussy.

Her breasts rose and fell in agitation and he realized one of her pasties had fallen away, leaving a succulent pink nipple exposed to his hungry gaze. Her hair was wild and free and her eyelids were blinking furiously. Her nose had reddened and he knew she was a breath away from sobbing her heart out.

No time like the present to place his call to Blaine fucking Bradford. They would be on the ground for at least an hour while the plane was refueled and new flight plans filed. Since her phone remained in the bathroom, he got his phone and dialed Bradford's number. It was burned into his memory. He probably recited the digits in his sleep.

"Bradford."

One ring and the asshole answered. He must've been expecting Dominic's call.

"I have your sister. You return my documents and my initial investment, you get her back unharmed."

"You have Livvie?"

"Yes."

Silence.

Dominic gritted his teeth. The asshole had hacked into his company's servers and stolen proprietary information *after* Dominic had bought into Bradford's company. "My files. My money. Your sister," he reiterated. "A fair exchange."

Bradford hooted with laughter. "Ride her until you think you've gotten your money's worth then consider yourself repaid."

A strangled moan came from Olivia and Dominic looked at her. She couldn't replace her hurt and shame with her glare fast enough. Dominic still saw it.

"I'm giving you three days to change your mind. Don't let your arrogance get your sister hurt." He clicked off the phone, hoping those parting words gave the man food for thought.

The anger and shock warring for first place in Dominic Luca's stunning features might've been hilarious if not for Liv's dire straits. Trussed, naked and at the man's mercy.

She'd tried to take a last stand. Or two. Maybe three. The number of times didn't matter—she'd failed at each and every attempt. If only her stupid phone had worked when she'd locked herself in the bathroom.

Then what?

They'd been in flight and he could've decided to pump her body with bullets rather than shoot the lock off his bathroom door. She hadn't even known their destination to give to the police but she hadn't been able to remain so passive. Anger had overruled fear and common sense. If he was going to take her out, though, she wanted to take something along with her. Preferably his balls. No, his entire package.

Now that he'd contacted Blaine and heard the truth, she wondered what he intended. At least Blaine hadn't implicated her and told Mr. Luca of Liv's hacking. She was up to her eyeballs in Blaine's schemes because of her own demands and she needed to make sure Dominic Luca remained ignorant of her role.

Of course she couldn't go to the police. Blaine might not have said anything to Mr. Luca but the cops were another story. If shit hit the fan, it would be her word against her brother's. She could say Blaine insisted she hack into the server but she'd made the choice to do it. If the police were brought in, he'd borrow fingers to point at her to make sure everyone focused on her activities and not his.

Mr. Luca scrubbed a hand over his eyes and his jaw clenched. Liv realized his eyes were a true blue, with not a speck of black or gray or green—just a beautiful blue. And they were studying her, contemplating her every feature, every slope and angle of her nude body.

Liquid heat rushed to her center and she squirmed, her nipples tightening. Her arms were stretched above her head, her legs spread, her ankles tied with the sashes she and Garth had intended to use. The props he'd helped her to choose. It seemed almost a betrayal to him that Mr. Luca was using them on her.

On the heels of that thought, humiliation rose in her at the thought of Garth, at the memory of Blaine's words and at the vulnerable position Mr. Luca had her in. She tugged at her restraints and the thin band cut into her wrists. Pain shot through her.

"If I untie your hands, will you behave?"

His voice washed over her. Since she wasn't a masochist and he intended to do her grave harm, her body shouldn't be so aware of him. But it had been from the moment she'd seen him. Garth had become inconsequential, as if he'd never been a part of her life. Considering how he'd belittled her a little while ago, perhaps, Liv's immediate attraction to Mr. Luca was a good thing. Despite how much she craved stability, lacking steadiness didn't make or break her.

"Will you?"

She nodded, the truth. She'd behave because she had no one to swoop in and save her. Her heart cheered at the thought that Garth had found out about her past and had dumped her before they slept together.

Though he arched a brow in clear skepticism, Mr. Luca leaned over her and began loosening the restraints. His scent swirled through her, cologne and scotch. With his tie removed, she glimpsed his strong neck and a small expanse of a smooth, tanned chest. Her hands were released and the blood that had stopped flowing rushed back through her veins. A thousand pins prickled her skin and she groaned, rubbing one wrist and then the other.

He took her hands into his and circled where the bonds had left red marks. The feel of his thumbs on her skin sizzled through her entire being. His profile was bold and sharp as he bent closer to her. The golden highlights softened his features and her insides melted at his nearness.

She wanted him and understood base desire. She'd seen what it meant to lack it and just fuck for profit and she'd felt it when Garth had kissed her. But just a glance from Mr. Luca or the sound of his voice made her ache for his touch.

"Is your brother that heartless?"

He'd kidnapped her as retribution for Blaine's actions. With her mouth still gagged, the most she could do was narrow her eyes, hoping he got the message: *that was a dumbass question.*

He chuckled. "Of course he is. This is Blaine fucking Bradford we're talking about."

He caressed her cheek with the back of his hand.

Liv tried to remember the last time someone had touched her with such gentleness. She and Garth kissed but she already knew her boyfriend—*former boyfriend*—had a kinky side. They'd planned on role-playing and experimenting with positions. Whenever they'd kissed, he'd wrapped his fingers around her hair and pulled and tugged and maneuvered.

Mr. Luca slipped her gag down, resuming his circular motions on her wrists. He sighed. "What am I going to do with you?"

Liv winced as another idea occurred to her. Her mother had used her body to obtain money to feed Liv. Liv could certainly use her own body to achieve her freedom.

She closed her eyes, ashamed of her wayward thoughts. She wanted better for herself. She licked her lips. "Release me."

His thumbs slowed but didn't stop. "That I won't do."

"You can send me to Blaine piece by piece and it won't make a difference. He's not going to cave and give you what you're demanding."

"Is that so?"

Liv nodded, hopeful because she had his full interest. Perhaps she was finally getting through to him. "I'm his half-sister," she explained. The thought to bargain her body in exchange for her release rose again in her mind. He was beautiful and masculine and she wanted him. "He doesn't care."

"What does he care about?"

"His horses. His cars. His money. Money, period."

"No girlfriend?"

"He's his own Alpha and Omega. I'm sure he's found a way to suck his own dick and swears he does it better than anyone else."

Her words caught up to her the moment Mr. Luca halted the delicious feel of his thumb and laughed, a real, true laugh that transformed his features from stunning and stern to beautiful and boyish. She giggled, nervous and aware and drawn to him.

As his laughter died away, his gaze roamed over her body again and she bit down on her lip.

Intensity filled his blue eyes. "How old are you?"

She hesitated. He was about thirty. A five-year age difference would be acceptable to a man like him. He was sophisticated, wealthy and ruthless and he'd want to surround himself with sophisticated, beautiful women whereas Liv hadn't even started college yet. With all the frequent moves, her grades had suffered so scholarships had been out of the question. The summer before she graduated from high school, she'd discovered her mother had cancer. Mom had fought a valiant fight but it took her life and took her away from Liv.

A man like Mr. Luca wouldn't understand all she'd endured in her twenty-one years. She'd grown up faster than she should have, seen and heard things she never should have. If he thought her a little older, he might treat her better. Sometimes, she wondered if Blaine was so nasty to her because he knew she was only twenty-one.

"How old are you?" he repeated.

"Twenty-five."

He seemed surprised by her answer and studied her for a moment, before gliding his fingers through her hair, massaging her scalp. "Just a baby."

His warm breath caressed Liv's ear.

She'd never been one to practice a reasonable amount of caution. Why start now when her life was unraveling?

"If we make love, will you let me go?" She'd negotiated the past two years of her life with Blaine. She could negotiate with Mr. Luca. She wished she could claim that logic as her sole purpose for offering herself to him. It wasn't. He gave her a wild, primitive feeling, unlike any she'd known before. Her life had always been very fluid, lacking real stability. As she'd gotten older, she'd learned to seize the moment.

A sexy half smile curved his mouth and he nipped her lips. "Why don't we make love to find out?"

"I need an answ—"

His tongue rimmed the shell of her ear and his touch sent tingles through her. He released her hands, skimmed her breastbone, before finding the exposed nipple and tugging at it. His mouth covered hers, his tongue slipping past her lips. He caressed her recesses, the warm, wet pad of his tongue tasting and teasing, plunging and ravishing. Fever invaded her body and she returned his kisses with the same fervor with which he'd bestowed them.

His fingers roamed across her belly, down to her inner thigh, before settling between her legs to caress her pussy, opening her slickened lips and massaging her clit. She moaned against his mouth, her eyes closing. One hand clutched his biceps while the other explored the silkiness of his hair.

A finger slipped inside her and he paused. "You've never made love before?"

"No."

Her answer seemed to satisfy him and a small smile creased his lips before his mouth met hers again. Instead of exploring her depths, he concentrated on her clit, coaxing her to release. Her climax hit her with stunning force and she pushed her sex against his hand, rocking against him and wiggling one of her ankles free.

He didn't give her a chance to catch her breath, didn't give her a chance to consider she'd just allowed a stranger full access to her body, just as her mother sometimes had done. He rolled on top of her and one of her ankles flexed in freedom, though the other remained tied to a slat. He rocked his erection against her, the material of his pants dragging across her sensitive flesh. She groaned.

He pulled his hips back. When he pushed against the juncture of her thighs again, his cock was exposed, the tip right at her entrance. His features were grim and determined as he buried himself inside her.

She cried out, her body tensing around him, gripping him. He was thick and huge. His gaze caught hers and he found her clit again just as he swept his mouth over hers. His tongue mimicked his cock, sliding into her and gliding out.

The manipulations of his fingers on her clit eased her pain and his movements. He was bringing her to the brink again, demanding a response from her, and she gasped, not understanding the sensitivity of her body. The overpowering feeling slammed into her again and she shook as she came around him, the physical release leaving her weak.

He lifted himself up, resting his weight on his elbows, and pumped into her. His assault on her body was so new it left her breathless. This man, whom she'd known mere hours, inflicted agony and ecstasy to her being. It appalled her that she wanted all he could give her and as much as he could give her. Instead of pushing him away, she gave in to rapture. His body stiffened and he jerked inside her before she felt the rush of his seed bathing her womb. His breath puffed out of him and he rested against her for a brief moment. He kissed her forehead, then withdrew from her and sat on the side of the bed.

She stared at the wide expanse of his shoulders, the hard planes of his back, the hollow dip of his spine. He stood and his taut buttocks greeted her.

In a lifetime filled with awkwardness and vulnerability, she'd never felt more awkward or vulnerable than she did as she watched him pulling up his pants and fastening them.

He faced her and his blue-eyed gaze roamed over her without a hint of the passion they'd just shared. "Let's see if this will make a difference to your brother."

The coldness of his words brought her abruptly back to her predicament and the realization that she'd given herself to him before completing the bargaining she'd began for her release. At least, her mother had always used her body with a clear purpose. Liv had just submitted in reckless surrendered.

He stared at her, as if he knew he'd taken what she'd offered and still held the upper hand.

"He might not care one way or the other that I gave you what you wanted when I fucked you. Then, again, he might take his dick out the ground and realize the seriousness of the matter."

"Er…" she squeaked around the dryness in her throat. His indifferent tone made Liv flinch. She had no idea what her next move should be. With determination, she shoved her regret and panic away—and her unaccountable disappointment. Not in the act itself or him particularly, just in the circumstances of the act. For a moment longer he waited and she knew he'd not add anything to soothe her discontent, if he even noticed at all. Which she doubted.

Not when he sauntered away, leaving Liv to stare in bewilderment at his retreating back.

CHAPTER THREE

*D*ominic sat near his bedroom door and stared out at the enveloping darkness, deep in contemplation. High in the sky, amongst the stars and the heavens, he usually felt as if he could do anything. Attain everything. Conquer the world, friend and foe alike.

They'd been airborne for just over an hour, about the same length of time it'd taken him to turn into a cruel, heartless bastard toward an innocent young woman. As if taking her virginity under the circumstances weren't bad enough, he'd had to score his parting shot. Like any of this was her fault. Whatever his reasons for seducing her, he didn't have to tell her the callous explanation of why she'd lost her virginity to him. He could've allowed her to continue to believe in whatever hearts and roses women associated with lovemaking.

But he wasn't a hearts-and-roses type of man. Who needed roses when he had money? Those were the exact words of the first woman he'd ever been stupid enough to consider his "girlfriend".

None of the women he'd ever fucked had been virgins, so he should've had the fucking sense to treat Olivia differently in the aftermath and not tell her he'd given her what *she'd* wanted, making it clear that bargaining sex for her freedom wasn't in the mix.

He wondered if she was experienced enough to realize the bullshit in his words. He'd wanted her from the moment he'd seen her on that stage. Hopefully, at twenty-five, she understood men better than what her virginity hinted at.

A virgin at twenty-five. Dominic hadn't thought much about it when she'd told him her age and then he'd discovered her virginity. But given her beauty and her desire to be fucked, it mystified him now.

After he'd considered all the dynamics, Dominic tried to fathom the huge apology he owed her. The problem was he didn't know how to fix his mouth to say he was sorry for the way he'd treated her.

Not quite knowing what he would say, he'd returned to the bedroom after being assured they were cleared for takeoff. He found her asleep, no doubt exhausted from her battle with him, not to mention losing her virginity. He'd had to call Felicia so she could meet them at the airport with clothes for Olivia since he'd ripped her dress and thong, leaving her with nothing to wear when they deplaned.

Despite their loose arrangement, Dominic knew Felicia well enough to pick up on her less-than-pleased attitude when he'd told her why Olivia Bradford needed new clothes. For some reason, he'd brushed off fucking Olivia as part of his revenge, not appreciating Felicia's enjoyment once she'd gotten the details.

His life was his business. When the time came, he'd marry. In the meantime, Olivia was just a casualty of her brother's bad judgment. Blaine fucking Bradford's sister had no long-term place in his life.

Still, the thought of hurting Olivia any more than he had turned his stomach. He rubbed a hand over his face. What the fuck had come over him? He didn't know her well enough to care about her and he had absolutely no reason to lie to Felicia *or* explain his actions to her. She was his personal assistant, the woman he'd dated in college and a woman who'd fallen on hard times last year then contacted him for employment after they hadn't spoken in almost seven years.

No matter. She was still a woman and he slept with her on a regular basis, though he'd made no commitment to her, a fact of which she was aware. Felicia was...convenient. His many business ventures left him no time to cultivate a relationship. It was expedient to escort her to her operas and symphonies straight from work then make love to her afterward.

He and Felicia had drifted apart in college, just as he and the women in the next two relationships that followed had. They were the only three "relationships" he'd been involved in and he kept himself detached.

Everyone believed he was too immersed in his work to commit. The truth of the matter was, he couldn't bring himself to do it.

Now he had a jealous woman on his hands. And a young woman he'd seduced.

Seduced because...he could. They wanted one another and there'd been nothing impeding them from proceeding. The thought arose that she hadn't really wanted him. Perhaps she'd felt she had no choice in the matter.

Kidnapped. Bound. Gagged.

He cringed.

So what the hell was he supposed to do with her? Keep her, fill her with his child, and walk away? Dominic had been so blinded by rage he hadn't stopped to consider if his actions would achieve the desired results. She was related to the enemy. Case closed. In his father's rules of business, Olivia was as much of a foe as her brother, whether she'd participated in the crime or not.

A phone rang and Dominic frowned. The happy-go-lucky tune certainly wasn't his shrill ringtone. Comprehension dawned and he realized it was Olivia's phone. He reached for it, having gotten it from the bathroom a bit ago and setting it on the seat she'd occupied earlier.

The word *Asshole* flickered across the screen. Curious and amused, he answered.

"So you do have her?"

"Why the fuck would I lie to you, Bradford?" Dominic growled, in no mood for the asshole's games. *Good identifier, Olivia.* He often referred to Bradford in much the same manner. "If you wanted fucking proof, you should've fucking asked to talk to her when I called you earlier, you fucking idiot."

"Fuck off, Luca," Blaine snapped. "Besides returning your files, how fucking much do I have to fork over to get her back?"

Dominic straightened in his seat. "How the fuck much did you steal from me when you hacked into my company after I'd bought into yours?"

"Listen, asshole. I don't have all the money you invested. I had...bills. But Livvie's nosy fucking friend hasn't heard from her and all hell is breaking loose. Livvie's boyfriend is accusing her of deceiving him about her social status. I guess she's a Bradford after all. We do whatever we must to get ahead."

He laughed and Dominic gritted his teeth. He didn't appreciate this asshole comparing himself to Olivia. "You do realize I'm withdrawing my partnership from Bradford Industries?"

"I can't believe you're going to leave my company hanging for some stupid files and the nickel you invested."

Dominic frowned. The asshole couldn't be serious.

"I'll give you some credit for the plans I unveil so we can both make a fortune. I already have a buyer," Bradford continued.

"Haven't you ever heard it isn't good to bite the hand that feeds you?"

Bradford sighed. "Damn it. I need money. I couldn't wait until your plans were implemented in hopes that my company begins to turn a profit again—"

"Then you forged your company's financials."

"No, I didn't!" Bradford huffed out a breath. "I tweaked my personal assets, so I made Livvie—"

"Leave your sister out of this." Dominic's guilt grew as he remembered the disapproval of the audience at the auction. Bradford had been using Olivia to get an easy ride. "Her involvement in your dealings ends now."

"I beg your pardon?"

"You heard me. I don't understand why you used Olivia but she doesn't need to be involved in your schemes."

"She involved herself!" Bradford flared. "She's so determined to get a college degree. How the fuck was I supposed to pay for it without money?"

That explained a lot. Such as how someone as strong-willed as Olivia could be talked into navigating society on behalf of her brother. She wanted an education.

"I need Livvie back, Luca," Bradford cut in. "She has to deal with her boyfriend Garth, and Karen is threatening to go to the police *and* the media if she doesn't hear from her. They were going on some vacation. So I need the little bitch back here to get her fucking friend out of my hair. I don't need the police or the media snooping around."

Dominic just bet the asshole didn't. Who knew what skeletons would surface. The rest of Bradford's words settled in and he gripped the small phone. "Olivia has a boyfriend?"

"Olivia *had* a boyfriend," Bradford corrected. "She's a social-climbing gold digger just like her mother was. She was our family maid, you know?"

"If he cared about her, he wouldn't give a fuck if she was as poor as a titmouse." He snapped the words before he thought better. But, so far, he liked Olivia, and he hated to think she'd be looked down upon because of circumstances out of her control. Namely, her birth and whether she'd been born the daughter of a maid or not.

"Livvie is a reckless little fool. Garth Walters wanted a few fucks from her. Who could blame him? Not many red-blooded men would pass up the opportunity to have a twenty-one-year-old beauty like my half-sister."

Dominic choked. "What did you just say?"

"Not many men—"

"Not that, Bradford. You said she's twenty-one."

"She is."

"That...Olivia told me she's twenty-five."

Bradford snickered, grating on Dominic's temper. "No. I assure you she's twenty-one. I'll never forget the day my mother held a cleaver to my father's balls when she discovered one of our maids was pregnant by him. He's lucky he got away intact. That auspicious occasion took place almost twenty-two years ago. Olivia is twenty-one and she just turned twenty-one."

What difference did her age make? It was only four years. But fuck...she'd just turned the legal age to drink.

"Again, Luca, how much do I have to fork over to get the inept wench back?"

He needed to throw out a number the weasel would be willing to fork over from Dominic's money and send Olivia back. His conscience warred with how he'd annihilated his enemies his entire life. If he sent her away, she'd be the fuck out of his life and he would've recouped some of his losses. It would be a compromise.

No. Absolutely not. Compromises were for weaklings. He'd stick with his original plans.

"You have three days to get the entire fucking amount you stole from me."

Not waiting for Bradford's answer, Dominic hung up.

The sound of a clearing throat broke through the contemplation of his morals and his sanity. Olivia stood before him, wearing one of his white dress shirts, which hung on her slender frame. Her hair fell around her in a wild tangle and her lips were swollen and red from his lovemaking. Now that he'd satisfied his animal urges and used her body to work out his rage toward her brother, he saw how young she looked.

He marveled at her strength of character under the circumstances. Other, more mature women would have crumbled by now. Kidnapped. Tethered naked to a bed, then losing her virginity to a total stranger. Who was this young woman and from where did she learn to deal with whatever came her way?

He rubbed his eyes and leaned forward, elbows on knees, and studied her. A true enigma.

"Where are we going?"

The huskiness of her voice sent desire pulsing through him. He supposed he owed her an answer. Somehow he had to find a way to rectify the wrong he had done and disregard how his father would've disapproved of his sudden conscience over a business rival. Following his father's lead in the company had never failed him. He remained on top of the business world and brought in more money than he knew what to do with. Problems arose when tried and true methods were disregarded. Dominic didn't like problems and he didn't like change.

"Dominic?" Olivia called softly and he realized he had yet to respond.

"Charleston," he said. "To my home."

She chewed on her lower lip and the image of her wrapping her lips around his erection rose in his head. She looked at her toes and shifted her weight. "Are you into BDSM?" she said, raising her gaze to meet his.

He lifted a brow, staring at her swollen mouth, at the softness of her eyes. Her black hair formed a curtain around her, a stark contrast to her ivory complexion and his white shirt she wore. The memory of being inside her made it difficult for him to remain where he sat. He wanted to reach over and touch her. Caress her. Take her.

"No," he answered, recalling her question when her dark brows furrowed. "I'm not into that lifestyle. I am, however, into doing whatever the situation calls for."

"And the situation called for me being tied up while we made love?"

Dominic looked away, unable to meet the confusion in her steady gaze. Guilt gnawed at him but he shoved it aside. He wanted what Bradford stole back. He didn't want a pair of stunning green eyes, a headful of midnight hair and a flawless complexion to sway him. He nodded, a brusque movement meant to deter her questions.

As if.

"Tell me a little about yourself," he ordered, the perfect way to put an end to her queries.

She eyed him with suspicion. "What do you want to know?"

Dominic shrugged, not caring to explore his need to know everything about her and not willing to admit it to her, either.

She wrinkled her nose, glanced at him, at her toes, and then at the window next to him. "I...my mother...Blaine's father...he was my father, too."

"Your mother was a maid," he blurted to make her explanation easier.

She bristled, her nipples pressing against the fine material of the shirt she wore. "I see you and Blaine discussed more than the terms of my return while you spoke just now."

"A little more," Dominic agreed.

"Why did he call back? I heard the phone and his special ring."

Ah, so that's what had brought her out. "Your friend is concerned about you."

"Karen?"

He hated the way she hooded her eyes, shutting him out.

"She shouldn't be. She won't be once she discovers I'm a bastard Bradford with no pipeline to an inheritance."

She pursed her lips. He wanted to un-purse and nibble on them.

"Not every wealthy person is so shallow." Was he? His parents had been. He'd never considered *not* marrying someone outside of his socio-economic class. Therefore, any shallowness he did or didn't possess had been a non-issue. "Did your mother have any other children?"

"No."

"Where did you grow up?"

"Nowhere in particular," she said carefully. "We were always on the move. Momma would...would—"

Lifting a brow at her, Dominic searched her face, studying the pink rising to her cheeks, the cool control in her green eyes. She shoved some hair behind her ear.

"Would what?"

"Shoplift," she snapped. "Get arrested for prostitution. My father would bail her out, do whatever rich people do to make problems go away, then we'd be off to the next town."

"Wouldn't it have been easier if your father just gave your mother money?"

"If he was still alive, you could ask him. Better, ask Blaine one day. He seems to know the reason behind everything our dad did. On the other hand, I have no clue why my father did what he did. Until he died, he sent me a new laptop every year but refused to give us money for the basic necessities of life."

"Makes sense that he'd give you the equipment," Dominic offered. She didn't look hurt and affronted by his matter-of-fact words. Her failure to fall to pieces over her lot didn't surprise him. In the short time he known her, he'd recognized her amazing resiliency. Her courage impressed him. Even though she shrugged at his observation, he wanted to comfort her. It couldn't have been easy for her growing up lacking money for simple provisions and only receiving a fucking yearly computer to let her know her father remembered her existence. That must've been...Fuck! What had come over him? She'd survived. End of story. Besides, she could've done worse and not received anything from Bradford. "The computer division of Bradford Industries made sterling products at one time."

Instead of answering, Olivia straightened. He wasn't a man in touch with his emotions, willing to soothe someone in a time of distress. He was cut-and-dry and only knew how to offer what he'd received growing up—detachment.

"But you were able to get an education?"

"By some miracle. Yes."

"And now your brother is paying your tuition to attend college?"

Her features turned inscrutable and she nodded, the movement guarded. "Yes."

Her wariness intrigued him. He wondered what he was missing.

She swallowed, waited a moment. Lifting a brow, he leaned back, indicating he'd follow her lead.

"Am I to share your bed as part of your revenge against Blaine?"

The moral, rational part of his brain told him to tell her no and to apologize for taking her virginity under the circumstances. But the lascivious male and scorned business partner demanded he tell her yes. He couldn't afford whatever instinct that made him notice Olivia's moods. In three days, he'd take whatever repayment Blaine sent to him and return Olivia. He would've exacted revenge, and to maintain respect, Dominic knew it was imperative to make an enemy pay by any means possible. It had been one of his father's golden rules. Ignoring the smallest infraction undermined a man's worth. As a result, Dominic had followed in his father's footsteps and steamrolled anyone who got on his bad side.

It's what set him apart from everyone else and kept him a winner. He was able to separate the aspects of his father's personality that he'd admired from the ones he detested. He'd appreciated his father's no-nonsense, hard-nosed attitude in business. On a personal level, he'd despised the man's cheating ways and the cold manner he'd had toward Dominic's mother. On the other hand, his mother was not much better. She'd had her share of affairs and remained in the marriage for money. As husband and wife, they were a joke. As parents, they were distant.

Dominic stayed away from relationships and had only cultivated one friendship—with the man who'd become VP of the company once Dominic took the reins.

"Mr. Luca?"

He started and scrubbed a hand over his face. Whether or not her brother was a motherfucker, she didn't deserve to be caught between them. She'd done nothing but been in the wrong place at the wrong time. Unfortunately, if he released her now Bradford would think he bested Dominic. And he liked the fact that he'd been her first. He wasn't ready to give her up for reasons that had nothing to do with the fucker she was related to.

Weakling.

His blood ran cold at the unbidden memory of his father screaming that word at him. As a child he'd heard it so often, Dominic didn't know which memory his mind had drifted to. As a teenager and adult, he'd learned not to be a weakling.

"Mr. Luca?" she repeated.

She continued to amaze and amuse him. After what had taken place between them, she called him *Mr. Luca?* She hadn't bothered to ask him if she could go into his closet and take one of his shirts but she couldn't call him by his given name? "Call me Dominic, Olivia. You've earned the right."

A rush of pink stained her cheeks and neck and she tiptoed forward.

"You don't have to worry about my men. The carpet is soundproof and the door between the sitting room and main cabin is closed."

She sat on the edge of the seat and her flush deepened. "It isn't that," she mumbled.

"Then what...?" His voice trailed off. She looked ready to erupt into flames. Of course. She was sore. What a supreme clusterfuck. "Never mind."

"You were big," she confessed. "You and Garth are vastly different in length and width."

Why the hell it should matter to him she'd seen her boyfriend's cock, Dominic wasn't sure. But the thought he wasn't the first naked man she'd seen up close and personal irritated the shit out of him. He couldn't even bask in the glow of her compliment about his size. He glowered at her. "I didn't realize you had any relations with this Garth."

"He...I-I mean...*I*...um...*sucked* him."

Jealousy burned through him and he leaned back. His hands balled into fists in his lap. So many thoughts ran amok in his head he couldn't focus on any long enough to form a reasonable response.

Jealousy? He'd known her how long? Certainly not long enough to be envious of a man whose dick she'd blown.

To prove he remained in control, he unzipped his pants and pulled out his cock, spreading his legs apart. "Come here."

He thought she might refuse or maybe his conscience would overcome his lust and stop him. To his immense relief, neither happened. A heartbeat after his order, she stood, took the step to reach him and then dropped to her knees. She wrapped her fingers around him, just above where his hand held on to the base. She leaned into him and dragged her tongue across his sensitive tip. Just as he had imagined, she wrapped her lips around him and slid her tongue along the underside before traveling up, trailing the thick vein running the length of him. He growled, grabbed a handful of her hair and thrust his dick into her mouth. She sucked in air through her nose, drew him in deep, her tongue swirling around him, the back of her throat massaging his cock head.

His balls drew in and his grip on her hair tightened. He pushed a final time into her mouth and exploded, anchoring her head in place to make sure she swallowed every drop of his cum.

Rising to his feet, he lifted her and set her on the chair, her ass facing him. Her pussy dripped with moisture and he inserted two fingers into her, circulating her juices, dragging them upward toward her ass. She had such pretty, firm cheeks.

The crack of his palm resounded in the silence. She jerked and cried out. His red palm print on her lovely skin heightened Dominic's libido, sending his dick into fuck mode. He slapped the other cheek, eliciting the same response from her.

He lifted her off the chair and carried her to the bed, keeping her face down and bent on the edge, her ass raised for his easy access. "Don't ever, *ever* suck another man's cock again."

The thought infuriated him and he slapped her ass again, and was rewarded with a rush of wetness seeping down her thighs. He wiped her cream away and coated his cock with it before delving into her pussy again. He spread her essence to the tight hole between her ass cheeks and she moaned. The sound earned her another crack. The only available lubricant was saliva and the arousal from her cunt. Using her pussy juice and the spit in his hand, he massaged his hard dick, pushing aside the frisson of guilt. Only wanting to possess her completely, this fearless girl who gave herself to him as if he'd courted her as a romantic interest. He didn't believe in romance, though. He only believed in lust, animal attraction, and pure instinct.

Once he coated his cock, he slid a finger into her forbidden area, stretching her, while the other finger worked inside her pussy.

He poised at the entrance of her ass, still massaging her cunt, his thumb working her clit. Her breath came in short pants and he knew she was close. Her inner muscles clamped around his finger and she pushed against him, trembling as she fell apart.

"Dominic!"

His name sounded so fucking sexy falling from her lips while she was in the throes of her orgasm. He cupped her pussy, his thumb caressing her bud as he inched a finger into her ass. She groaned, arched against him, and he slipped farther into her. He gritted his teeth, her little moans driving him insane. He continued caressing her sex, not wanting her to descend from the heights of her orgasm until he'd breached her ass, determined to erase the thought of any other man, especially Garth.

Garth.

Dominic growled and surged into her, flicking her clit faster and faster until she came against his hand again. He gripped her hips and began moving inside her.

"Look at me."

She turned her head to the side and he bent forward, taking her mouth in a hard kiss. His tongue ravished and ruled, his cock pumping into her ass. His chest pressed into the elegant line of her back, her damp, dark hair brushing against his nose, tickling his shoulders. He lifted himself, threw his head back and thrust one final time into her. His cum burst from him in a wild rush, leaving him weak and weightless.

And utterly and completely confused about why he couldn't get enough of Olivia Bradford.

Inside a limousine, Liv listened to Dominic talk to his assistant, a pretty blonde about his age. Felicia had been waiting at Charleston Executive Airport and she'd boarded the plane to deliver a pair of jeans, a white t-shirt and a very pretty bra and matching underwear set and wedge sandals for Liv.

The woman hadn't had much to say but her disapproval of finding Liv in Dominic's bedroom and dressed only in his shirt was apparent. Liv didn't owe an explanation to anyone, since her current predicament wasn't her fault in any way, shape or form.

Hearing Felicia and Dominic's camaraderie, Liv wanted to get away from the resentment and jealousy goading her. Dominic had taken her virginity, asked her to perform oral sex on him, breached her most forbidden place and spanked her. Now he acted as though she didn't exist.

Liv tightened her fingers across her belly. Whether she wanted to admit it or not, her current predicament *was* her fault. She'd repaid Blaine for the money he'd squeezed out for her mother's hospital care, chemo and subsequent funeral through her tears and sweat by cooking and cleaning for him. Her anger and grief and desire to rise above her start in life had urged her to ask Blaine to pay her tuition to college. Her GPA had dropped so substantially during her mother's illness Liv had lost all hope of getting scholarships. She'd laid her cards on the table and Blaine had laid his. In the end, he'd had the royal flush because *he* had the money.

It wasn't until she was well on her way to a prison sentence by agreeing to Blaine's request that she crack Domamill's IT servers that her brother confessed he needed the information in those files so he could turn them into cash—money to keep Bradford Industries afloat and pay her tuition.

A burst of sound caught Liv's attention, Dominic's husky laughter combined with Felicia's flirtatious giggle. Anger burned in the pit of Liv's belly, her body still throbbing from all that Dominic had done to her. She might've acted like an experienced sex goddess last night, infused with adrenaline and hope and a galling fascination with her captor. Like an excessive amount of alcohol left her with a telling hangover, in the light of day, her loss of virginity told on her. Her ass hurt. Her mouth hurt. And her pussy hurt. Most of all, her feelings hurt.

She shifted, staring out the window at the passing scenery. Not much to see, she realized. Just miles and miles of trees interspersed with fields and unidentifiable bodies of water every now and then.

She could confess to her role in this entire fiasco and ask Dominic for the chance to reverse what she'd done. She peeked at him through her lashes. Sunlight angled in and he looked like an angel, illuminated in sacred light. Everything about him glowed—golden hair, golden skin, blue eyes. He was a mortal man, though, flesh and blood and too handsome for words.

"Olivia!"

The impatience in his voice alerted her he'd called her name several times. She swung her attention to him. "Mr. Luca?"

The fact she addressed him as "mister" didn't seem to bother him. Their sex fest should've removed such formalities but she'd refused his suggestion she call him Dominic. With Felicia present, he seemed perfectly fine that she didn't use his given name. Why that rankled, Liv didn't know.

"We're taking you to my house. But Felicia has informed me I have several pressing matters, so I will leave you in the care of my bodyguards."

He indicated the two men with a nod.

"I suppose I have to service them too?" she snapped.

Felicia smirked at her and Liv narrowed her eyes at the other woman.

"Of course," Dominic said, his voice a purr, so matter-of-fact Liv wanted to tear his eyes out. "If you wish to be responsible for their castrations, go ahead and service them as much as you want."

The two men stiffened, so she knew they'd heard, but they didn't say anything.

She, on the other hand, scowled at Dominic and spoke her mind. "I didn't mean that and you know it."

"Do I?" he asked coolly.

She didn't want to have a private conversation with such a captive audience. She wanted to tell him she was afraid he would make her sleep with whomever he chose just to get back at Blaine. Though she'd suggested their sex, hadn't he seized the moment and done all sorts of things to her as revenge against her brother rather than true desire for her? Didn't that mean he could offer her to whoever he wanted and expect her to comply? After all, she'd acted just like a whore. Just like her mother.

The thought made her cringe and she shied away from it. The observation was completely abhorrent to her mother's memory. Connie had taught her to survive and survive Liv would. But she wanted to tell Dominic if she had to pay with her pound of flesh, she only wanted it to be with him. She plucked at her t-shirt.

"What am I supposed to do while you're gone? If you don't want them to tie me up and throw me in some dark, hideous place, you will take them with you." So her imagination was running away. It always had when she took time to consider something unappealing. On the way to his house with his girlfriend present and without so much as a small acknowledgement to their sex, Liv's fear returned, despite her best efforts to pretend it hadn't been her companion since Dominic had taken her. "What else am I supposed to think otherwise?"

He glared at her. "I don't have dark, hideous places in my home, Olivia. Please get a handle on that wild imagination of yours. Am I clear?"

She glowered at him.

He turned to her and drew her face between his thumb and forefinger. "Listen to me, Olivia, and listen well because I don't make a habit of repeating myself. These men work for me. I trust them with my life, so I trust them with yours. If they want to hurt you, they may as well blow their fucking brains out now because to touch you, other than to carry you from danger, is to sentence themselves to death. Am I clear?"

She nodded.

"As to what to do, the staff has already been instructed you'll be my guest for the next three days. They'll know what to do until I return this evening. You're free to explore my house. Understand you'll be shadowed anywhere you go on the premises."

Huge live oaks offered shade while the magnolia trees with their big white flowers perfumed the air. Yellow jessamine, azaleas, rhododendron, roses and honeysuckle gave his grounds a colorful, artistic feel, the blue catmint bushes bright against the red foundation of his house. Dominic wondered at Olivia's first impression. Frowning, he turned to look out the back window as the limo headed back down the driveway, watching as Albert and Howie ushered her up the wide steps and through the mansion's front doors. The same question plaguing him all night reared up again—what the fuck was he going to do with her?

As if he didn't know. He'd already done exactly what he'd wanted to do with her from the moment he'd glimpsed her on that stage. It was what he'd continue to do with her until she left.

That is the reason you instructed Mrs. Dobbs to put her in your room, isn't it?

"Nic?"

He straightened in the seat and swung his gaze to Felicia.

"We are still attending the symphony Saturday night, aren't we?"

Saturday was five days away and by then Olivia would be gone. He and Felicia could return to their arrangement.

Fuck. Since falling into bed with her two months after she'd started working for him, he'd tried to accept Felicia as the woman in his life. She was very good at what she did, reliable and kept his appointments on track. She'd missed a half day in the eleven months she'd worked for him. But he kept backing away, unable to enter into the same type of loveless union his parents endured.

He didn't believe in love one way or the other. Eventually, he intended to marry and provide heirs for the family business as his father and grandfather had done. With Olivia, however, he felt different. He wanted to know more about her. Her ability to adapt to whatever situation she found herself in fascinated him. At the auction, she'd kept her head high. When he'd kidnapped her, she'd remained collected and when he'd fucked her she'd responded with passion.

Of course, she had Blaine Bradford for a brother. On the surface, she was the asshole's complete opposite. Once Dominic got to know her, he might discover her to be as duplicitous as Blaine and as money-hungry as Dominic's mother.

The thought brought his good sense back. There was absolutely no chance in hell he and Olivia could be anything more than what they were. He only knew her in the biblical sense and he'd keep it that way. Any guilt he felt toward taking her virginity had been removed when he discovered she'd sucked her boyfriend's dick.

Besides, she was carrying around a bag filled with sexual items. She wanted to get fucked, so he'd obliged her.

He'd continue to oblige her as long as she remained with him.

"Get Bradford on the phone," Dominic growled, coming to a quick decision. Olivia had to go. He didn't want to continue to use her for sex and he damn sure didn't want to frustrate himself trying to have something more with her and thus set himself up for a caring relationship only to suffer disappointment. "Tell him to meet me at his office as soon as possible. Tonight would be excellent. I'm giving Olivia back. She shouldn't pay for his crimes when she had no involvement."

He didn't miss Felicia's expression turn to one of relieved satisfaction, sure it was because he intended to return Olivia.

"I have to meet with Clark. After that, I'll have my driver bring me home so I can await confirmation of my plans."

She patted his thigh and leaned forward, indicating he not disturb himself by lifting the phone and relaying the message to the chauffer. Felicia made herself useful at every turn. Once she'd explained Dominic's intentions to the driver, she leaned back. "You slept with her."

Her accusation wasn't phrased as a question and he clenched his jaw to hold in his surging irritation. "Yes. I'm sure you were already aware of that since you found her in my bed."

She released a sharp breath, her honey-colored eyes hardening. She was elegant and sophisticated, but her cool manner reminded him of the way his mother had treated his father. "I can't wait to see Bradford's face when you tell him you've fucked his sister."

Yes, just like his mother. As long as fucking another woman served a purpose, other than satisfying lust, Felicia didn't care who he slept with. That annoyed the fuck out of him. "You aren't coming. Olivia will be humiliated enough without you being there to witness it."

"You're awfully protective of her for this to have been just a revenge fuck."

"She's a twenty-one-year-old girl, caught in a battle between her brother and me."

"Which you overlooked or rationalized in order to justify taking her to bed."

He had no answer to that because she was right. Felicia was gorgeous with her peaches-and-cream complexion and pale blonde hair. She had it swept up, revealing the graceful curve of her neck and the perfect lines of her features.

"I'm sorry if I've hurt you or betrayed you," he said tightly, wondering what the hell else he could say.

She cocked her head. "Are we in a relationship, Nic?"

"No. We're just us."

She swallowed and gazed out the window. "If you compared me and Olivia Bradford, who would meet your standards as the future Mrs. Luca? Who have you confided in the most? Me or her?"

Neither. He told Felicia just what she needed to know to get the job done and held shallow conversations with her outside the office. He'd told Olivia less than that.

"Who do you want to confide in? Me or her?"

Olivia. The thought came to him automatically, though he barely knew her. He wasn't sure why he felt he could trust her more than he did Felicia. But remembering her clipped words as she had spoken of her mother and her guarded hesitation did something to Dominic. She was a fighter but oh so vulnerable. Perhaps that was it. He saw through Felicia's guile, whereas all he saw in Olivia was innocence. He'd felt her innocence, taken it, lost himself in it.

He wanted to discover what made Olivia different. Why she pulled at his heartstrings, his libido, his humor.

"What traits do we have that you like?" she continued.

She expected verbal responses but he didn't intend to provide any. If she wanted to amuse herself questioning him while he remained silent, so be it.

He liked Felicia's organizational skills and her no-nonsense demeanor. On the other hand, he liked Olivia's fire and passion and loved the way she made him smile. He wanted to know more about her and wished they'd met under different circumstances. As it stood, he didn't see how they had any hope to have a chance of a relationship.

"Who can you see as mother to your children?"

Olivia. For all he knew, she might be well on the way to being the mother of his child. His plan to send her back to Bradford pregnant hadn't been well thought out but had already been implemented when he'd fucked her without protection.

So now what? He and Felicia took precautions against pregnancy, on his end as well as hers. It was the smart thing to do for both of them and he'd never consider putting Felicia in the vulnerable predicament he'd put Olivia in. Did he really expect her to raise his child alone? Besides, a pregnancy would hurt *her*, not her fuckhead brother.

She had to go back to the asshole. Dominic knew he wouldn't stray from the course he set if she remained. It wasn't in him to suddenly shift directions. If he had his choice, he'd murder Bradford and be done with it. He didn't. The asshole was in hiding, therefore Dominic only had Olivia to use as his instrument of revenge.

"I'm thirty," Felicia said, breaking into his confusion. "I'm ready to settle down and nurture a family. This girl has her whole life ahead of her. A lifetime of experience to gain. This is the twenty-first century, Dominic. Most twenty-one-year-olds aren't thinking marriage and motherhood. You're *ten years older* than this girl. So not the 'in' thing nowadays. It would be much better if it were reversed. Cougars are all the rage."

"I get your damn point, Felicia. I'll arrange for her departure as soon as Bradford calls. When I return her, if he doesn't turn over my files and money, I'll take it out of his ass as I'd intended to do in the first place."

She smiled and he grimaced, turning his attention away from her. His attempt to think of the meeting he'd shortly attend failed. Instead, a pair of green eyes filled with a mixture of emotions monopolized his thoughts and he cursed.

The first sign things were awry was when Dominic walked into the entrance hall and saw Howie standing next to a long ladder right beneath the huge chandelier. Craning her neck, Mrs. Dobbs was wringing her hands. The next sign came when Dominic heard Albert's frustrated voice, along with a series of clanking noises.

"Get down *now*, Miss Bradford. Mr. Luca has staff to do the cleaning."

"Of course. I heard Mrs. Dobbs." Olivia's voice was muffled.

When Dominic stepped forward, he realized why. She stood on the top tier of the ladder, on her tiptoes, holding a bowl. With deft movements, she was unhooking the crystal teardrops of his chandelier. Her hair shone like polished ebony and Dominic itched to run his fingers through the heavy mass.

"But I'm here and I have nothing to do," she said.

When she stretched farther up, Dominic's heart skipped a beat, right in tune with the collective gasp of his three employees.

"You're going to fall and break every bone in your body, ma'am," Mrs. Dobbs pointed out. "Please, please, for the love of holiness, get down."

"No." *Clank. Clank. Clank.* "Your concern would be heartwarming if it was for me," Olivia said dryly, "and not because you're worried about what Mr. Luca would do if I were to break my neck."

"Miss Bradford," Howie began through gritted teeth, using his weight to keep the ladder in place. But he was too far down to be of any use if Olivia slipped. "We're concerned about both." The man was diplomacy personified.

"Please get real. I do this work at my brother's house and no one watches out for me."

"Get down, Olivia." Dominic strode forward, adding his voice to the chorus of others, and brooking no argument.

Olivia squeaked in surprise and yelped when she lost her balance. The crystals—his very expensive crystals—went flying, pinging to the marble floor. Olivia went airborne, falling backward, her terrified scream echoing off the walls, her hair flying around her. He was too far away to reach her and he swore he aged ten years in those few moments. By some miracle, Howie and Albert caught her, although the force of her fall sent the three of them sprawling onto the floor. The men's chests cushioned her head and upper body.

After checking to make sure his men were uninjured, he pulled Olivia to her feet. The dazed look in her eyes made him wonder if she hadn't hit her head, after all.

"Are you okay?" he croaked, pressing her head against his chest. Her heart pounded in a furious beat, matching the pace of his. The scent of his bath soap on her skin hit him in the gut.

She stared down at her hands and he saw the blood oozing from a cut on her palm. He reached for her injured hand but she pulled away.

"Yes, I'm fine. No thanks to you. I didn't know you'd returned so your voice was the last one I'd expected to hear." A frown creased her brow. "What are you doing here?"

Besides almost keeling over from a heart attack? "I live here."

She rubbed her hand on her white shirt, smearing it with blood. "You have a very beautiful house."

"Thank you." Noise around him indicated members of his staff were beginning to clear Olivia's mess. "Are you sure you're okay?"

She shrugged.

"It wasn't so long ago that I dropped you off. Do you always manage to get into such mischief?"

The question seemed to drag her from her stupor. She spun on her heel. "I'm not a child," she flung over her shoulder, running toward the staircase.

A few moments later, he heard a door slam. He'd deal with her in a moment. "You two," he said, pointing at Albert and Howie. "In my office. Now."

CHAPTER FOUR

*L*iv ran cold water on her hand, rinsing away the blood and searching for a glass fragment, though she didn't believe she'd cut her hand on one of the crystal teardrops. Instead she thought she'd scraped it against one of the metal edges of the ladder steps.

Her entire life had flashed before her eyes as she'd fallen, the faces of the people who'd had the most impact on her sliding through her head. Her mother's kind features and her father's handsome profile. Her brother's smirk. The way Karen's eyes crinkled when she laughed. The dimples in Dominic's cheeks when he smiled.

If Albert and Howie hadn't caught her, she would've been dead. And who would've mourned her loss? Maybe Karen. What a sad commentary on her life. But her mother had been her best friend and they'd moved from pillar to post, just to survive. They'd never remained in one place long enough for Liv to form bonds with anyone. Just when she'd settled into one school, they'd move again and she'd have to get used to another.

No regrets and no running, Liv.

Such a hard task. She better understood why her mom so desperately wished she'd had the ability to change certain things in her life. Maybe, instead of pretending she didn't wish for a steady childhood, Liv could commit to having a stable future. She'd already chosen her career, whereas before her mother's illness Liv hadn't had a clue on her prospects.

She took the bar of expensive soap, the same kind she'd used when she'd soaked in her bath not long after Dominic dropped her off, and lathered her hands, wincing at the burn. This certainly didn't have anti-bacterial agents.

Such soap was too ordinary for a bathroom with cut-stone tile floors, gold tone accents, and an island in the middle of the floor. It had wood borders framing the doors and separating the walls from the ceiling and floor. The bathtub served as a divider between two vanities. Liv stood at the one that didn't have Dominic's toothbrush in the holder with a bottle of mouthwash and tube of half-empty toothpaste next to it.

She couldn't invade his personal space, as much as he'd already invaded hers. Her heart fluttered at the thought of his lovemaking and she chewed on her lower lip, contemplating her next steps.

The hot soak had soothed Liv's aches and pains. Once she'd dried off and re-dressed herself in the clothes Felicia had delivered on the plane, she'd attempted to explore, wanting to find a computer. But his two guard dogs were on her heels and she hadn't been able to escape Howie or Albert. Resigned, she'd started back up the stairs when she'd heard Mrs. Dobbs directing the staff on what needed doing.

Liv hated idleness—one reason Blaine insisted she try out Tai Chi and Zen. He thought the activities would be a good way to channel her energy as her work for him wound down. Liv believed he'd wanted her more focused to get the hacking job completed quicker. As if his reasons mattered. Liv couldn't focus enough to engage in either Tai Chi or Zen while under house arrest, and had thought it a good idea to busy herself while she awaited Dominic's return.

She'd overheard Albert and Howie talking about the exact nature of Dominic and Felicia's relationship. It seemed as if they were a couple and the bodyguards surmised the other woman wouldn't appreciate Liv's presence. If the roles had been reversed, she wouldn't have appreciated her presence either. They'd gone a bit further and bet "Luca" would return Liv sooner than the three days once Felicia put a bug in his ear.

Liv ignored how upset the thought made her. She'd offered Dominic pussy and he'd taken her up on her proposal. She hadn't even gotten the chance to bargain their sex in exchange for her release. She'd hinted and he'd pounced. It hadn't mattered that he had a girlfriend who, from the sound of it, he cared enough about not to want her totally unhappy with Liv's extended stay.

The soft thud of a closing door alerted her to Dominic's presence. She hadn't closed the bathroom door, so she could hear anyone entering the master bedroom quite well.

She grabbed a hand towel from the stack in the wicker basket atop the island then patted the dampness away, satisfied to see the blood had stopped. She started toward the bedroom just as Dominic appeared in the bathroom doorway.

"Felicia isn't my girlfriend in the strictest sense of the word."

It shouldn't have shocked her to learn his two spies had caught on to what had so upset her, since they were paid to spot every minute detail of their surroundings and the people in contact with their boss. On the other hand, Dominic addressing it with her surprised her.

"I didn't know there was another definition when sex is involved and the word relationship is bounced about." She scooted past him and headed for the wing chair on the other side of the room. The barley-twisted four-poster bed drew her attention and she pictured Dominic and Felicia on it, fucking. Quickly she glanced away, stumbling the last step to the chair.

Dominic's bedroom featured a blue and brown scheme and windows overlooking the marsh.

Her desire for Dominic caused all kinds of heat to assail her. She was convinced she could melt an ice cap if she sat on one. Perhaps the air temp wasn't low enough or maybe her emotions were in overdrive and heated her body. It was cool in the house and Liv hoped the air from the overhead vent would help calm her.

Impossible with Dominic so near.

His eyes smoldered and Liv's body responded to his close proximity with shameless need. She couldn't seem to get enough of him. Despite her recent deflowering that caused her lingering soreness, she felt herself moistening.

He stood in the midst of the expensive furnishings, wearing his wealth like a badge of honor, his charisma and sexuality as lethal as weapons.

"Your relationship with Felicia doesn't matter. I'm in your life for the time it takes Blaine to return your property. After that, I'm gone and you can get back to the woman who isn't your girlfriend in the strictest sense of the word."

What a perfect opening to make her confession. She wanted Dominic to hear her reasons for her actions in her words before Blaine put a twisted spin on the events and portrayed her in an even worse light than what her crimes would show her to be. She opened her mouth to speak the words then snapped it closed. Maybe she could get away without Dominic ever knowing. Why taint his opinion of her any more than it was?

"Olivia—"

"What does it matter?" she reiterated. If she confessed, Blaine might very well turn his back on her completely and it would be years before she got to college. "I don't know you so it doesn't matter. I'll be gone in three days."

He remained silent for a heartbeat. "Are you in love with your boyfriend?" he asked after a moment filled with mutual awareness and deep tension.

Perhaps the question would sound out of left field to most, but Olivia believed she understood why Dominic asked. He must be in love with Felicia but, like Olivia, had enjoyed their lovemaking. Love had little to do with the demands of the body. As much as she wanted to shout that, yes, she had someone she was in love with too, she couldn't.

"No. I like him. Or I did. But he deserted me too."

He paced in front of her. "The way we met...the way I took your virginity...there's no way for us to ever have a relationship under those circumstances."

More than how he'd taken her virginity stood between them. "Look, Dominic, I've been exposed to Blaine and the twisted workings of his mind for months. You don't have to explain why you did what you did. I already know. So please stop pretending you have a conscience. You and Blaine are cut from the same cloth."

He stared at her as if he'd never seen her before. "You honestly believe I'm like Blaine fucking Bradford?"

Her eyes widened at his appalled tone and then she burst out laughing. "You really believe you aren't?" she asked around her giggles.

He shoved his hands in his pockets. "Not in the least."

She shrugged. "I can't change your perception of yourself."

He crouched in front of her and she combed her fingers through his hair, straightening the strands determined to remain astray.

"Who are you?" she whispered.

"The scion of a wealthy family whose parents cheated on one another for as long as I remember."

Olivia stilled her fingers at the bitterness in his voice and the resentment in his eyes. She touched her forehead to his, kissing his nose. "Perhaps that's why you're so jaded?"

He pulled away and rose to his feet. "What would you know about that?"

"A lot." She sighed. "More than I should. My momma had me at twenty. We sorta grew up together." she reasoned aloud. She drew her eyebrows together. It didn't make a difference that Dominic had grown up wealthy. His environment sounded as unstable as hers had been, only in a different way. After all, money didn't make good parents. Morals did.

Thinking farther, she imagined herself as a mother. One look at Dominic and the useless offer she'd made him to obtain her freedom and she knew she'd already fallen short in the morals department. Her mother had, too, but that didn't mean Connie hadn't been a good parent. Olivia would be too. She'd teach her kids about love, trust and loyalty. She'd live in her own truths so they could live in theirs. She'd show them fairness and hoped they learned it in return.

He shoved a hand through his hair and Olivia decided to back off. She wasn't stupid enough to believe she'd ever see him again after he settled things with Blaine. Her life just didn't work that way and it mightn't ever.

"H-how long have you and Felicia been a couple?"

"We aren't a couple. We're just us. I've known her since college. When I gave her a job last year, I hadn't seen her in seven years."

"I think that's rather sweet. College sweethearts reunited and making a life together."

He grimaced. "If you say so. I'm returning you to Blaine as soon as possible. I'm waiting to hear from him and when I do, we're flying back."

And with that, Dominic turned on his heel and left her alone, allowing Liv no time to consider if this new turn of events relieved her or not.

Dominic stood on his sunset porch, watching the dying rays of the day turn into evening's twilight. Night sounds echoed in the marsh beyond. The distant bellow of a gator. The splashing of a crane, swooping in to catch a fish. The croak of bullfrogs. He'd been home all day, conducting business, waiting for Felicia's call that she'd heard from Bradford.

Instead of contacting her about purchasing additional clothes for Olivia, he'd called the stylist personally and described Olivia to her, then ordered a black gown to replace the one he'd destroyed, a pair of slacks and a blouse, underthings, shoes and another pair of jeans and a t-shirt, since her blood had ruined the one she currently wore. Everything had been delivered an hour ago, while he ate supper in his home office.

He'd left Olivia alone, not wanting to tempt himself by dining with her or asking her what she thought of the clothes he'd purchased. As a general rule, women were the least of Dominic's worries. His relationships ended without much fanfare or drama.

Olivia comparing him to her brother rankled as much as her romantic notion that he and Felicia had reconnected. He saw her at the office every day. He had no one to rush home to, no one with whom to share his life or his wealth. No one who expected him to be faithful.

Perhaps it concerned him because he emulated his father in business and so he feared he'd do the same as a husband. He only knew he felt like a dirty motherfucker for the way he'd treated Olivia and it caused unfamiliar conflict within him.

A ray of dying light bounced off a dark head and Dominic watched Olivia trek down the long, wooden pier that extended out into the marsh. The evening breeze ruffled her gorgeous midnight hair. Another figure trailed behind her and he recognized Howie. She stopped and turned, beckoning Howie closer.

Dominic picked up a pair of binoculars he sometimes used to spot the marsh animals. Olivia's lovely face came into sharp focus. Even without makeup, she was breathtaking. Long and thick, her dark lashes ringed her green eyes. Her pink lips invited him to feast upon them for hours. He wondered what she was telling Howie, who nodded and gave her his undivided attention.

Dominic turned the corner to the north porch and raced down the steps, assuring himself he didn't want any surprises sprang on him. Olivia was too intent not to have something up her sleeve. He mightn't have known her long, but he already knew that determined look. The one that led to chaos.

He reached them within minutes. He smiled at the brightness in Olivia's eyes and the relief on Howie's face. "You and Albert rest for the evening. I'll look after Miss Bradford."

"Yes, sir." Howie's mumbled, "Good luck," reached Dominic on the evening breeze.

He folded his arms and stared down at Olivia, waiting for an explanation.

"You must have a boat," she began.

"And?"

"I would love to go through the marsh at night with nothing but the sounds of nature surrounding me."

"And you suggested that to Howie?"

She nodded. "But he said he needed to ask you and pulling the boat out and getting everything together should be started in daylight."

"There are gators out there."

"I know. Isn't it exciting? I've never seen a real live alligator up close."

"You wouldn't worry about the danger just the adventure," he responded in amusement. She was impulsive like that. Her stomach growled and he frowned, losing the tiny bit of lightness blooming inside of him at her zest for new experiences. He was always so contained and controlled with every action he made carefully planned, the exception being taking her when he hadn't been able to find her asshole of a brother. She was a free spirit, something akin to a wild, little fairy. Some of that magical dust must've swirled into his brain. Gritting his teeth, he abruptly ordered his thoughts back to realism. "Did you eat?" he asked harsher than he meant to.

Not taking offense at the return of his assholery, Olivia wrinkled her nose, an adorable, endearing gesture. "I wasn't hungry."

Another growl indicated otherwise.

"How about we put off your swamp tour to another time while I find you something to eat?"

She didn't resist when he took her hand and began escorting her toward the sunset porch.

"I didn't leave the house through this entrance," she said.

"You should have. This is the sunset porch. You get the most amazing evening views."

"I suppose you have a sunrise porch," she surmised with sarcasm.

"Yes. As well as a north porch, a pergola and a pool terrace." Since they were back at the north porch, Dominic decided to escort her the circumference of the house. Each porch connected to the next one. When they reached the sunrise porch, he let them in through a sitting room and guided her to the kitchen.

The chef stood at attention when he saw Dominic. The sous chef and dishwashing staff stopped their tasks and fell into line.

"Miss Bradford will be my guest for a day or two."

He hadn't heard from Felicia or Bradford yet and Dominic wondered if the man would call at all. Bradford had already told Dominic to ride Olivia until he'd felt he'd been repaid. On the other hand, Bradford had also said he needed his sister back, so Dominic believed Bradford would be happy to have Olivia returned sooner rather than later. Still, someone had to pay. With Bradford acting as such a self-preserving coward, there was only one person left to use as retribution. Olivia. He'd known her under twenty-four hours. Despite his mind-boggling attraction, the amount of time he'd been acquainted with her and with his intentions to send her back, he didn't have any reason to chance a lifelong way of dealing with his enemies, in the form of a pregnancy.

"Make sure she gets whatever she likes to eat," he continued on that bleak note and nodded to the chef. "Please send a tray up to my suite, along with a bottle of red wine."

"Certainly, Mister Luca," the chef responded, his expression not changing.

Within a half hour, the cook sent up enough dishes to feed Olivia and a battalion of men. Freshly fried shrimp and catfish. Hot cracklin' cornbread. Smoky turnip greens. Fried okra. Warm peach cobbler.

While Dominic held out his glass to have the wine poured, an empty plate was set in front of Olivia, and he nodded at the maid.

"Do you drink?"

"What do you think?" she asked with a giggle.

"Please pour Miss Bradford a glass of wine."

Once the woman complied, she stood next to Olivia, waiting for directions on what to serve her. Olivia sipped her wine and waved the maid away.

"Thank you," she said. "But I can't decide what I want so I don't want to take you away from your duties. It looks very good."

Dominic signaled the maid to leave. "When did you last eat?" he asked Olivia, once the maid had gone.

"Sometime yesterday before the event."

Dominic rose to his feet and piled a little of everything onto her plate. She sipped more wine but refused to pick up her fork. He picked up a piece of catfish and held it to her lips.

She opened her mouth and he slid the crispy fish inside. She closed her lips around his finger and gave him a small nip. The last thing he needed was her flirting. In his current mood, he'd never be able to resist her. Determined to fight against the lure of her, Dominic fed her another piece. She licked the juice from his finger, snapping his shaky resistance.

"Do you want food or my cock?" he asked roughly, draining his glass.

She licked her lips, picked up her glass and drank from it before placing the rim at his lips. He lapped the residue she'd left behind, his gaze never leaving hers.

"Can't we pretend we didn't meet the way we did? Just for tonight?" she whispered.

He should tell her no. Walk away. He didn't want her head filled with romantic nonsense. Then again, she knew where they stood. That's why she'd asked for tonight only. He wouldn't be using her or mistreating her if she'd approached him to fuck her.

"Oh hell, yeah," he murmured, drinking more of her wine and then kissing her to allow her to partake of it. His tongue swept into her mouth, the liquid seeping down her throat. "What do you want, Olivia?" he demanded again. "Food or my cock?"

"Your cock," she responded, reaching over to grip his dick.

Sucking in a breath, he stood and lifted her into his arms.

He fused his mouth to hers, tasting her sweetness, and groaned. She smelled of his soap, wine and warm, vital female. He told himself he was giving her what she'd asked for, taking what she offered. He placed her on his bed and decided not to waste time, undressing before he climbed next to her.

Her gaze fastened on his groin and his cock swelled further beneath her scrutiny. Dominic gathered her into his arms, glad she was still fully dressed. He intended to worship her body as he bared her. A soft, tentative stroke touched him and he jerked, goose bumps traveling along his spine.

"Don't pretend you haven't been up close and personal with cocks," he growled, her hesitant caresses maddening.

"Not cocks," she hissed. "Only one."

"I beg to differ. According to you—"

She cupped his balls and Dominic gritted his teeth, almost missing her words.

"According to me, it was only Garth, whom I thought was my boyfriend."

She stroked the length of him from base to tip then closed her hand around the head, circling her thumb. Dominic drew in a breath.

"I sucked Garth and only Garth. Is that clear enough?"

His nostrils flared. "Why the fuck are we having this conversation?"

To shut her up, he captured her lips again and tugged up her t-shirt, baring her midriff. He lifted her long enough to remove her shirt, leaving her in a sheer, mint-green bra embroidered with macramé. He kissed his way down her belly to the waistline of her jeans. As he unfastened the denim, he continued to kiss her, lave her fragrant skin. She sighed and the sound whispered through Dominic's nerve endings. He hooked his fingers in her pants and slid them down her long legs, leaving the matching boy-cut panties in place. Her triangle of hair tempted him through the sheer material and he spread her legs wide. Kissed the inside of her thigh. Bit gently. Sniffed her pussy, breathing in her heady scent. He slid the seat of her panties aside and nosed her. Her lips were slick and swollen. Holding her delicate flesh open, he rubbed his cheek across her clit, his stubble of hair dragging across her wet, sensitive bud.

She groaned and lifted her hips. "Please."

He removed her panties.

The jealous thought Garth might've used his mouth on her rose in Dominic's head, driving him crazy. He blew on her clit, began a slow thumbing. Her body was taut as a bow, begging him to lick and suck...to gobble her up. He pushed two fingers into her, her drenched cunt deepening his arousal.

He kissed her mound. "You like having your pussy licked?"

She trembled and her breasts rose and fell, her nipples beaded against her bra. "I-I've never had it licked. Garth said—"

Dominic growled, a territorial right possessing him. He opened his mouth and claimed her, his teeth nipping her clit, his tongue slipping into her pussy. She screamed, coming almost immediately, but Dominic was merciless, determined to erase *him* from her head. He clutched her buttocks, gripping each cheek in a hand, and swiped his tongue over her clit until he was almost drowning in her juices. He tongued her until he was nearly out of his mind with his need for her. His name tore from her mouth, a broken sob.

Dominic rose up and buried himself in her tight body. Being inside her was like soaring amongst the stars. She was so responsive to him, so hot for him. Her cream drenched his mouth and chin. He took her lips, filling her with his tongue and her taste. She anchored her feet on his hips, open and exposed to his thrusts. Her green eyes were glazed with passion, dark with lust and desire. When he pulled his hips back, she thrust hers forward, canting her pelvis to meet the demands of his cock. Her uninhibited response brought out a wild fervor in him. He slammed into her, their mouths fused, the scent and taste of sex an aphrodisiac.

He couldn't hold back his cum and it gushed from him, pouring into her. Each time his cock jerked inside her, more of his seed slid into her womb. He pulled out of her and rolled over, spent. Without asking his permission, she rested her head on his arm, snuggling against him.

He kissed the top of her head, wondering if she wanted to talk and praying she didn't. After-sex cuddling wasn't something he did.

"Dominic?"

"What, Olivia?"

She raised a sleepy-eyed gaze to him at his rough tone. Her skin was flushed and she'd never looked more beautiful. He tucked her closer and pulled the covers over them.

"What?" he asked, a little more gently.

"Can Howie show me around Charleston? I've never been and when we return, I can help to cook or clean or whatever you need me to do."

"Slow down, Olivia. You do know a security detail is assigned to you?"

She pouted and sniffed. "You can keep Albert. I'll take Howie."

"Is there a reason why?" When had he become such a jealous jerk? But something about the fondness in her voice as she said the man's name.

"I like Howie. I don't like Albert. He's always so stern, not once smiling. He's worse than Blaine."

"To answer your question about who will show you around Charleston, that'll be me."

Her eyes widened in surprise before she lowered her gaze and fell silent.

"I grew up there." He'd liquidated his parents' assets upon their deaths in a plane crash eight years ago, wanting no reminder of his childhood. Did it make him cold that the tears he'd shed upon learning of their deaths had been followed by a wave of shame? His father would've scoffed at his tears and Dominic felt he'd dishonor the man's memory by exposing his emotions. His mother might've comforted him or she might've shrugged away his feelings. Since then, he'd never once mourned them. He'd resigned himself to his duties and forged ahead, accepting that they were gone. He didn't like thinking about that awful time because he didn't have awful times, so he continued talking to Liv as if thoughts of his parents and the house he'd grown up in hadn't sent a twinge of hurt through him. "I promise I make an excellent tour guide."

When she remained silent, Dominic wondered what was going through her head. Her body was still as taut as a bow and he'd already learned a quiet Olivia boded ill. "All right. Cough it up. What are you thinking?"

She shrugged out of his hold and sat up, rising to her feet, her hair cradling her face, shoulders and back. When she turned, he got a full view of her wearing the pretty bra and nothing else. The triangle of black hair drew his gaze and he regretted when she grabbed her panties and put them on.

"I don't want my visit to Charleston ruined with interruptions and explanations." She combed her fingers through her hair and tossed it over her shoulder. "I want to have happy memories."

"I don't explain my actions to anyone."

She looked away before meeting his gaze. "Don't you? You were so determined to keep me for three days. Then you talked to Felicia and you changed your mind."

"What Felicia and I discussed is of no concern to you," he bit out. *How the fuck did she know anyway? Olivia hadn't been in the car with him and Felicia.*

"It's true, isn't it? That's why you're suddenly in a rush to get me back to Blaine?"

"If you must know, Felicia *did* make me realize it's best to send you back sooner rather than later."

He didn't like the accusation in her eyes and he absolutely detested how low it made him feel.

"So the fact that I fucked you had no bearing when I requested my release but Felicia pointing out a "few things"— she used air quotations to emphasize her point – "is the impetus you needed to let me go?"

Her voice was even, her stance straight. He stood as well, unable to keep his half-hard cock hidden, goaded by shame and guilt. Olivia had summed up the situation perfectly, except for one small fact. He wanted her gone because he truly liked her. Somehow, she made him think and feel and remember he was a man and not just the ruthless heir. He wanted to explore those feelings with her, but he knew he couldn't. Not under the circumstances. That wasn't to say they'd have a future together. Maybe, any relationship he might've pursued with her would've crashed and burned under normal conditions. But, under these? Where he wanted to pummel her fucking brother into the ground? Where he'd taken her virginity out of lust and anger and weakness?

And what if they had gotten to the point in their relationship where he'd proposed to, and married her? What then? She wanted an education. He needed heirs.

"Your non-answer is my answer," she said quietly.

He grabbed his boxers and pulled them on. "You're right. Howie and Albert should accompany you on your tour tomorrow. When you return, I expect you to enjoy my house. If you'd like, I'll have a massage therapist meet you here tomorrow evening."

"May I have my phone?"

She sounded so lost and forlorn. The fact that he caused either didn't sit well with him, but he'd see this through to the end. If he gave her the phone and she brought in law enforcement, he'd ruin his family's name. In that moment, he realized the revenge he sought again Bradford may turn against him. He sighed.

"The last time you possessed it, you threatened to call the police. Since your status hasn't changed and you're still, in essence, my hostage, you can't have your phone."

"I just want to call Karen."

"Your friend?"

She nodded.

He didn't want her so sad. Besides, he needed to make it up to her for allowing her to believe Felicia was the catalyst behind his decision to send Olivia back to New Orleans as soon as possible. Of course, he could always tell her the truth, but he wasn't stupid. Not entirely anyway, though his actions of the last day and a half begged to differ. In the short time they'd been together, Olivia had developed some type of attachment to him. Or, maybe, he believed that because he wanted it to be true?

"Please, Dominic."

Fuck, he couldn't deny her. He nodded. "I'll arrange for Albert to get her on the phone for you tomorrow."

Her smile was wide and she stood a little taller. "Maybe I want to go to Charleston to escape."

Her words held no conviction so he recognized her teasing. Smirking, he sauntered to her and gathered her in his arms, raining kisses along her throat. "Albert and Howie are prepared and equipped to handle any attempt you might make."

"Why are we arguing?" she asked in a soft voice.

Before Dominic could respond, she dropped to her knees and pulled his cock from the opening in his underwear. He drew in a breath when she took him in her mouth and began drawing on him, hard and deep, as if she intended to suck him dry. The soft pillow of her throat relaxed and she slurped him. Her tongue massaged the underside of his cock. The thought of her cream all over his shaft as she deep-throated him almost made Dominic explode. She sucked him until his knees grew weak. Dropping to the floor with her, he dragged down her panties, turned her around and rammed into her. He fisted her hair, moving in and out of her heat, controlling her movements by keeping hold of her ebony locks. He fell forward, covering her back with his body, taking her fast. Her vaginal muscles squeezed his cock and he gasped. She clenched around him again and moaned.

"Let it go, Olivia," he ordered. "Come on my cock."

She nodded and groaned, coming all around him, wild and hot and wet.

"Fuck!" he snarled before he pounded into her a final time and came in a hot torrent inside her.

Exhausted, they collapsed on the floor, Dominic careful to keep his weight resting on his arms and elbows. Before he moved, he unhooked her bra and she let it fall to the floor.

He guided her back to bed and the inscrutable look in those clear, green eyes before she drifted off left him sleepless for the rest of the night.

CHAPTER FIVE

*L*iv stared at the huge Pineapple Fountain in Waterford Park. The water rained down from the three tiers ringed with stone pineapples. Neatly cut hedges ringed the fountain, while a short distance away, the Cooper River flowed in placid contentment beneath the hot, Charleston sun. She wasn't sure what she'd been expecting when she'd asked Dominic if she could stay the full three days or what she'd expected when she requested she be able to sightsee.

A small part of her had cheered when Dominic made his offer, but he'd sounded so grudging and put out. Of course, he'd be both. He had whatever with Felicia and Liv was sure that whatever didn't include Dominic taking young women on carriage rides and an afternoon lunch. But neither did Olivia think Dominic's men particularly enjoyed their babysitting assignment and they gave her little freedom to just enjoy the beautiful day. She'd been floundering ever since she'd awakened this morning and found herself alone in Dominic's bed. Thoroughly, wickedly sated, but alone all the same.

She was used to being alone, so why fret about it now? Once she pulled herself together after the devastating loss of her mother, she'd been too busy repaying her debt to remember her grief and loneliness. In a way, Blaine's demands had been good. They'd kept her on the move, one step ahead of her sadness. She'd gotten a handle on her feelings and bottled them away, praying she never uncapped them. Once she'd met Karen and Garth, she'd just known she could shove her emotions in a dark corner and never face them.

But, just as her mother once warned, everything eventually caught up to a person. Liv supposed that included emotions.

A bird swooped by and Liv followed its progress for a moment. She smiled at its freedom and seeming carelessness. Liv had thought the charity auction heralded a new lease on her life. She'd thought she was free of Blaine if not free of her origins. Yet, here she stood, ensnared in Blaine's schemes because of her own desire to have what *they* had, that elusive one percent of Americans who had the world at their feet. Her desire to become a pediatric oncologist was real. If she hadn't been so determined to make Blaine recognize her as a Bradford and hand her some of what she felt entitled to, she would've applied for grants and student loans and work-study programs.

It would've taken her longer but she would've eventually gotten her degree and opened her practice. She would've one day been able to have a dining room and someone to serve her fresh fruit, creamy grits, crispy bacon, fluffy eggs, fresh-baked biscuits and strong, thick coffee as Mrs. Dobbs had done this morning for Liv.

After she'd completed her breakfast and was rising to take her dishes to the kitchen, Albert and Howie had strolled in with their earpieces in place, wearing dark suits to match their dark sunglasses.

"The car is ready whenever you are, ma'am."

That had been Albert, the epitome of manners after the bald-headed maniac had been yelling at her to get down from the ladder and ordering her to stay inside and not go on Dominic's pier. Howie might not appreciate her actions, but at least he didn't make her feel like a preschooler.

Without Dominic in the Escalade, she'd been alone in the backseat, left with nothing but her thoughts and her fears. Instead of wallowing in either or dwelling on the worry of what would happen once Dominic discovered she'd done the hacking in the first place, Liv kept a steady watch on the passing scenery. The sudden hard right had made her glare toward the back of Albert's head. She just didn't like him and she wasn't sure why. If Dominic had been a mobster, Albert would've taken pride in being a hitman. She just got that feeling about him.

Pockets of traffic along their route had slowed the drive down. It was thirty-five minutes before Albert was crossing the Ashley River then taking the Lockwood exit and heading for a ramp on Calhoun Street. Ten minutes later, Albert was turning into a parking area near Mid-Atlantic Wharf. As soon as the SUV was halted, Howie was ushering her out. She'd meandered along, trying to plan in her head what she wanted to see first. Then, a horse and carriage had clopped by, the driver pausing long enough to point out something to the couple on the seat. It had looked so romantic and all Liv could think about was Dominic being with her instead of his security detail.

Howie had guided her to Waterford Park and suggested they take the ferry to Fort Sumter. She'd asked for a moment to just enjoy the acres of waterfront beauty and they'd fallen a step behind her. Not too far, though. Never too far. If she decided to make a run for it, they could easily reach out and grab her.

Dejected now, she bowed her head and turned. "Dominic said you'd call my friend for me. I would appreciate it very much if you dialed Karen's number. I won't take long," she added when they hesitated.

Howie nodded and reached for his cell phone, but Albert raised his hand to stop the other man's intentions.

Liv swallowed at the nastiness she detected brewing beneath Albert's surface. She perceived the insult in the way he studied her lips and breasts, detected the cold calculations in his stare. Why she couldn't shake the feeling that he'd slit her throat and stab Dominic in the back, she wasn't sure. Maybe, it was her experience with cruel men. Not her personally, but watching her mother run across violent lovers from time-to-time. Unless she landed herself in jail, Connie had no one. But, then, Liv's father would come to bail Connie out, presumably for Liv's sake, so she wouldn't be completely alone, since he refused to take her and raise her.

Albert stepped toward her and Liv backed away. While she was under Dominic's care and in his bed, he'd protect her. She knew that too, as much as she recognized Albert as the snake that he was. "Dominic promised I could call Karen."

The mention of Dominic's name seemed to snap Albert out of whatever he'd intended. He blinked and his jaw clenched. "Excuse me, Miss Bradford," he clipped out.

He stepped away from her and pulled out a cell phone. Liv supposed he needed to hear from Dominic she had permission to have contact with someone in the outside world.

She glanced at Howie, who seemed puzzled by Albert's behavior. On the other hand, she just chalked it to the vagaries of men with too much power. In the scheme of things, Albert was a stinking little minnow in a vast sea of sharks. Unfortunately, because Dominic had given Albert power over Liv, she'd become the minnow and he the shark.

How depressing.

"Tell Clark the deal's off," Dominic snapped to the vice-president of his company.

His four executives and Felicia started. Her pen paused, her mouth falling open in shock.

"Are you crazy?" Preston Ellerton asked. "We've walked a fine line with the law for months to get this deal done."

"Then undo it."

"Nic, whatever burr is up your ass, get rid of it," Preston advised. "We've finally gotten the bastard where we want him. If we pull out now, we might never get a chance to work with him at our price."

"Nic, er, Mr. Luca," Felicia amended when Dominic narrowed his eyes at her. She knew better than to address him so informally at the office. "Mr. Ellerton is right. The company is in a vulnerable position. Clark is willing to let you in because he needs your backing. If he finds someone else, we'll lose the advantage."

Dominic had gotten into his position with Blaine because of this exact reason. Yes, Bradford Industries had been in dire financial trouble, but Blaine had quickly found a way to misappropriate Dominic's money. Now, not only did Dominic have a company bleeding money left and right, he had an asshole who'd gotten the best of him. Despite all the security checks and financial analysis, Blaine had still scammed him. Dominic had never quite trusted the bastard but he'd wanted to add Bradford Industries to his portfolio.

Instinct was telling him Clark wasn't much better. Not that he'd ever allowed himself to be had again. He just had too many other ventures at the moment and he didn't want the hassle of adding a floundering company with a prickhead as its president.

"The goddamn deal is off. Now, deal with it." He rose to his feet as his cell phone rang. Seeing it was Albert, he didn't hesitate to answer. The man had to be calling about Olivia. "Is there a problem?"

"Miss Bradford wants to call her friend, sir. I'm confirming with you that she has permission to do that."

Dominic turned away from the table and sauntered to the window. "Shouldn't she be on her tour at the moment?"

Albert's silence annoyed him as much as the memory of Olivia in his bed this morning did. She'd been so warm with his scent all over her body. Her dark hair had been spread across the pillow, lying against her cheek. She'd looked so peaceful, so right in his bed. He hadn't wanted to leave her. He'd wanted to take the day off and escort her around town, then spend the night in bed with her.

Albert sighed. "Sir, she doesn't seem to be enjoying herself all that much. We suggested we take the ferry to Sumter and she's just ambling around Waterford Park."

Much like he'd been ambling through the day. "Put her on the phone."

"Yes, sir."

A moment later, Olivia's musical voice chimed through the line. "I promise I'm not going to tell her anything. I just want to talk to Karen," she said in a rush.

"How's your tour going?" he asked gruffly. Despite her fast words, she sounded miserable, so very sad and alone.

"Wonderful. How's your day going?"

"Fucking terrible." And it had been going terrible since he'd made love to her this morning while she was half asleep and then left before she'd fully awakened.

"I'm sorry to hear that," she responded. "Is there a solution to whatever problem is making your day so terrible?"

Her genuine interest was a novel experience. He wasn't a family man so he didn't have a wife to call to soothe away his frustrations when something went wrong like the rest of the men in the office did. "The solution *is* the problem."

"Turn that around and make the problem your solution," she offered. "Sometimes they are one and the same."

How well he knew that. "This is your day to enjoy Charleston, Olivia. Do so. I promise you I will have Albert call Karen on your way back to the Island."

"Maybe I shouldn't have turned down your offer to show me around," she said quietly. "I would enjoy myself better if you were with me."

Her words shouldn't have pleased him but they did. Immensely. "Is that so?"

"Yes. I saw a couple on a carriage ride and it looked like so much fun. Then I thought about being squeezed against Albert and Howie and I changed my mind."

"Excellent decision."

Though he wasn't joking she thought he was because she giggled. His well-ordered, business driven life was falling to drops of shit around him because he couldn't resist her laugh and he couldn't resist her body.

"Go on the goddamn Sumter tour and learn a little about the war. Take your time. I'll be done here by the time you're finished and I'll take you to dinner. Have you ever eaten she-crab soup?"

"Um, no. What's in it?"

"The eggs from crabs. You'll love it."

"I can't wait to try it. I hope it doesn't taste like lox. I think lox is disgusting."

"I'll keep that in mind. And, no, rest assured, she-crab soup doesn't taste like lox."

She sighed, a tiny sound that made Dominic ache.

"I won't be able to work in peace if I think you aren't enjoying yourself."

"I'm fine, Dominic."

Her voice caressed his name. She rarely said it when he wasn't inside her but he loved the way her tongue wrapped around the syllables.

"I'm used to taking care of myself. Well, for the past thirteen months anyway. Since my momma died."

A well of tenderness opened inside Dominic and he smiled, remembering how she'd made him see stars with the kick she'd given him. If he'd been intent upon harming her, her way of taking care of herself hadn't been a very good idea, trapped on a plane as she had been.

"I won't be able to enjoy myself if I think you're worrying about me," she said.

"Then we're even."

"Where do they serve she-crab soup? Maybe I can stop in and try some for lunch. That way, you won't have to worry about me and I won't intrude on your day."

"Don't you dare do any such thing. You're not intruding."

She went silent, then she said, "Are we going to a fancy restaurant?"

"It's rather elegant."

"I'm not dressed for that."

"Olivia, are you purposely difficult?"

"No. Just practical."

"Fine, if we amend your schedule, would you agree?"

"Amend it how?"

"Instead of sightseeing, let Albert drive you to a boutique to buy a dress."

"I don't have any credit cards. I think I have about eight bucks in my purse."

"Have I asked you for a credit card?"

"No, of course not, but you've already replaced the dress you ruined. If Albert takes me home, I can just change into it."

"Olivia, I don't have time to argue with you. I'll let you decide if you want to go sightseeing or if you'd like to go shopping without restriction. Put Albert on the phone so I can tell him to follow your instructions on how the rest of your day should go."

"If I go shopping, I still need a place to bathe and change," she pointed out.

"If I take care of that, will you buy the fucking dress?"

She sniffed. "You don't have to be so nasty."

"Yes or no."

"Yes. I'll go buy a dress."

"And shoes."

"And shoes."

"And whatever else you need or want."

"Dominic!"

"Fine. I'll have a suite reserved for you. I'll meet you there this evening."

She squealed. "Do you still have my bag?"

The bag with all the sex books and ties and toys? Fuck yeah. "Yes."

"Can we use it tonight when we get back to the house?" she whispered.

And suddenly, Dominic's day brightened considerably.

CHAPTER SIX

ore designer labels were thrown at Liv than she knew what to do with. After almost two hours, her gaze kept returning to a gold dot miniskirt and the matching half-sleeve, sheer top. She liked the full swing of the skirt and the metallic bits on it. She chose from one of her favorite jewelry lines a Pyramid Ring, a Safari Dust Hinge Bracelet, and Encrusted Rhodium Spear Earrings, top of the line pieces she knew about from Karen and the websites they sometimes browsed when they visited each other. Karen had usually purchased. Liv had always fantasized. Until now, when Dominic turned the nightmare of a kidnapping into something out of a fairytale with his generosity.

"Are you sure you wouldn't like the python leather skirt?"

The asymmetrical design of the skirt and the angled zipper appealed to her. She contemplated adding it to her purchases but Dominic had already bought a couple of outfits for her. She didn't want to abuse his kindness. No one had ever spent money on her for no other reason than extravagance. That Dominic did made her feel special. Or...? God, had her mother's life of prostitution and thievery started like this? With a rich man doing nice things for her?

Stop, Liv. No regrets.

How could she not regret her enjoyment of her shopping spree when she thought of Connie? Although Dominic hadn't left her much choice in going with him, *she'd* attempted to instigate their sex the first time and had pressed for it again last night. She was freely and willingly enjoying his money. She...

No, no, no.

Putting her morals into question now would only make her realize the gravity of her situation. She doubted he'd do her any serious harm, but she was still a prisoner with Albert and Howie tracking her every move. Though he'd relaxed a bit, Albert still seemed the scarier of the two. No matter what he did, something about him just rubbed her the wrong way and she didn't doubt he'd do whatever he had to do to keep her quiet about her predicament.

She needed to pretend Dominic was spending money on her because he cared about her and not because of whatever may have led to his decision. When her ordeal ended she'd put her life back into proper perspective. In the meantime, she'd live in the moment and go along with whatever came her way.

"Ma'am, how about I add the skirt to your purchases," the sale woman pressed.

Liv shook her head. "No."

"Any of the skinny jeans? The lace dress? The cami tank?"

Liv wanted all of it but she didn't want to cross an unseen line between indulgence and avariciousness. "Please just bag my current purchases. Thank you."

Disappointment flashed in the woman's eyes before she pasted a smile on her face and nodded. "Yes, ma'am, Miss Bradford. Anything you'd like."

Once the items were wrapped, Liv reached for them but Howie materialized from wherever he'd been hiding and took them.

"We have a couple more stops, ma'am, before you can get to the hotel and relax until Mr. Luca arrives for you."

Liv frowned, ignoring the saleswoman's dreamy expression. "I think I have everything I need."

A cough alerted her to Albert's presence. "I'm sorry, ma'am, but Mr. Luca has instructed us to bring you to a shoe boutique and then, er..." His voice trailed and a red hue crept up his neck, crowning his bald head. He leered at her. "A lingerie shop."

"And wherever else you may need to go," Howie inserted.

Albert's look changed, to one of embarrassment as he faced the other bodyguard. Liv blinked, wondering if she'd imagined Albert's ogling.

She shook off her uneasiness and chastised herself for boxing him into an unsavory category because she didn't like him as much as she liked Howie.

She forced a smile. "All right then. I need to find a drugstore for shampoo, lipstick and nail polish."

The saleswoman released a huge sigh, either in disbelief or reproof. Liv couldn't tell which.

"Not to worry, Miss Bradford," Howie said with a small smile. "Mr. Luca is sending some folks over to do your hair and makeup. Now if you're all done here...?" He stepped aside so she could walk past.

With a last, covert glance at the items she was leaving behind, Liv nodded and departed.

∞ ∞ ∞

By the time Liv was shown to the suite, two hours later, she was exhausted. Then again, she'd tried on more clothes and shoes than necessary, lost in the sheer enjoyment of doing something she'd never done in her life.

Now she was in the luxurious suite, overlooking downtown Charleston, nibbling on the cheese and crackers that had been waiting for her along with fresh fruit and a bottle of champagne. Howie was sitting with her so of course she couldn't use the phone to call Karen unless she locked herself in the bedroom. As she considered it, the idea seemed more and more appealing. Locked in the bedroom, she could soak in a hot bath and then take a nap.

She didn't get a chance to do either because a knock sounded on the door. Howie answered and Albert led in four women. Liv was introduced to her hairstylist, makeup artist, masseuse and nail tech.

"Who is she?"

Dominic threw several folders into his briefcase and glanced at Preston. Though Dominic was six months older than Preston, his friend was already graying at the temples, outstanding in his sable hair. He had brown eyes and a ruddy complexion, earned through his love of watersports.

"Nic?"

Dominic had been working at a furious pace all day but he was still running an hour late. He'd grabbed a quick shower in his private bathroom and changed. He'd called Albert and set everything into motion for after dinner. He just needed a couple folders to look over once Olivia fell asleep later tonight. He leaned down, closer to the ultra-thin monitor screen, and double-checked numbers. "Who's who?"

"The woman who has Felicia's claws out and the one who has you rushing to get out of here."

Felicia's claws had been out all day. He supposed she was waiting downstairs in the car and would give him an earful on his drive to the hotel. He hoped Olivia wasn't angry and he prayed the carriage was there.

"Well?"

"Olivia Bradford." Why deny it when he was itching to see her? The thought that she was there at the hotel, waiting for him after he'd spent the day at the office, thrilled him. "She's been my guest for a couple days."

Preston whistled, drawing Dominic's attention. "And whatever the reason she's your *guest*, you better know what the hell you're doing. She's Bradford's bastard sister and rumor has it not his favorite person."

"What does that have to do with me, Preston?" Dominic growled, shutting down his computer. "Bradford has something I want. I have something he wants. We'll make an exchange and I'll be done with the whole matter, including Olivia."

Preston laughed. "I've never taken you for an idiot, Nic. You've been riding a high since you talked to her. I think you might be in—"

"Don't," he said. "I'm not *in* anything with Olivia other than enjoying her company." *Wrong, asshole.* He couldn't forget how far in lust he was with her. Just the thought of Olivia hardened him as if he were some horny, hormonal teenager. "Did it make me feel good to talk to her earlier? Yes. But this is a temporary arrangement."

"Have you slept with her?"

Dominic clamped his jaw and slammed down the top of his briefcase.

"That's a yes," Preston said dryly, brushing off the sleeve of his gray pinstripe jacket. "I've known you since college."

Dominic grabbed his briefcase and started for the door, reminding himself to stop down the hall to grab the charts and graphs he'd sent to one of the shared printers.

Preston followed. "Felicia is a great woman but you two are so fucking boring together. You didn't even...you just fell into whatever the two of you have because she's here. You knew her. She was your college sweetheart but I'm betting not your first love. I don't believe you've ever been in love so how the fuck can you recognize it?"

Ignoring his friend, Dominic snatched the papers from the printer and paused long enough to shove them into his briefcase.

"Come on, Nic. You've been immersed in this damn company for years. I don't believe you don't want a relationship. I just believe you've never given yourself time to pursue someone you might fall for."

"I pursued Felicia. And Kim. And Monica," Dominic snapped, naming the only three women he'd ever been seriously involved with. "It just didn't work out between us."

"So what happened? There's more than those three women to choose from. Why aren't you happily married with one or two little Dominics running around and getting lost in the marsh around your house?"

He reached the bank of elevators and punched the Down button. "I don't know, damn it."

"It isn't as if you're a philanderer. What you're doing now is the closest you've come to womanizing."

Womanizing? Me? How could that be when he wasn't in a relationship with either Olivia or Felicia. Dominic winced at the thought as the doors slid open and he and Preston stepped inside. The dynamics of his relationship with Olivia were no longer clear, if they ever had been. Explanations were not something he did because they had never been required of him. Preston pushed the button for the first floor.

"Don't let this opportunity pass you by," he said as they started to descend.

Dominic scowled. "Suppose I don't? What happens if *we* drift apart? She's in my house. If we float apart, what do I do with her? Throw her out? Send her back to Bradford?"

The elevator rocked to a stop and Dominic hurried out once the chrome doors slid open.

"Dominic, fuck! You're the extreme opposite of your father, you know that? You wanna know what you had in common with Felicia? And Kim? And Monica? The love of seeing your name on the goddamn *Forbes* list every year. The quest to have doors thrown open at the snap of your fingers." Preston thrust a hand through his hair. "Listen, man. Those who don't know I'm vice-president of your company develop a new attitude when they discover it. Being associated with you has opened more doors for me than I could have ever imagined when we met at football tryouts. And I'm not even fucking you. Am I saying these women are bad? No. They are all wonderful but they want what you represent, not *you*. That's why you've never warmed up to them. Even you, in all your blindness to relationships, have a sense of survival."

"Who's to say Olivia isn't the same?"

Preston stepped closer to him. "I understand she's been your *guest* and with the way you feel about Bradford, I'm using the term loosely. You've spent hours planning whatever the fuck you've been planning for tonight. When have you done anything close to this for anyone else?"

"What am I doing?"

"Rushing from the office at seven when you're here until midnight most days of the week. You've never spent a small fortune in one day."

Dominic started walking again. "I'm very generous to Felicia. I was very generous to the other two."

"Money is as money does. You showered them with gifts that stylist woman bought for them. You took them to all kinds of exotic places. You're paying Felicia much more than she deserves and you take her to those horrifyingly boring operas and symphonies every few weeks. La-de-dah. But you've never involved *yourself* in any other way. You've never had Albert call and report to you on the doings of any woman. You also ordered the man to return to the shops and purchase whatever Olivia left behind that she really wanted."

Dominic shrugged, reaching the entrance door to his office building.

Twilight turning into night and the cooling temperature promised a beautiful evening when he stepped outside. He couldn't stop his smile or the anticipation he felt knowing he was minutes away from seeing Olivia after his long day of meetings. Once or twice he had excused himself to call the restaurant, florist and carriage company. Tomorrow would be soon enough to warn his staff to stop the speculations about his personal life if they wished to remain with the company. Right now, he wanted to bask in his peace and tranquility.

His driver hurried around and opened the door for him. As expected, Felicia was waiting for him.

"Good night, Preston," Dominic clipped out then ordered the driver to start off without delay.

"Think about what I've said, Nic!" Preston's voice boomed through the closed door.

Felicia flipped on the overhead light as the car began to move. "Aren't you going a little overboard to rub Bradford's face in the fact you have his sister?"

"Stay out of it."

"Unless you come with me to my house right now instead of going to wherever with Olivia Bradford, you'll need to find another PA."

"Are you giving me an ultimatum?" But didn't she have that right? Despite the looseness of their arrangement, he'd never discouraged her from believing they suited for something more. But as she stared at him so calm and collected, he understood Felicia wanted what he represented and not necessarily *him*. That had been acceptable before Liv and would've continued to be after she left, if Felicia wasn't making a demand on him for all the wrong reasons. "Are you?"

"Yes! You can't let the girl come between our arrangement. What happens when she leaves? If you go out with her tonight, you'll be left without her and without me."

Dominic fell silent, refusing to give up his plans with Olivia to appease Felicia. If she wanted to leave her position with him, so be it. When he pulled up in front the hotel he was pleased to see the horse and carriage with a driver in red and white livery atop the perch.

"Bradford called." Felicia's words halted him.

"And?"

"He will meet you at midnight tomorrow at his office."

With a brusque nod, Dominic exited the car. "See you around," he said before he slammed the door.

Liv's worry that she would be late turned into concern she'd been stood up when five o'clock turned into six and six o'clock morphed into seven. She'd been waiting for an hour, staring at herself in the mirror, not quite able to believe she was really Olivia Bradford.

She rarely wore makeup, and when she did it was only lipstick. She had neither the time nor the money for much else. Although she was wearing some tonight, it was the dress's sparkly, sheer material that seemed to make her skin glow. The heels made her legs look endless and she twirled. She should try out for the catwalk, she thought with a giggle. At five feet seven, she might make the cut.

A knock came on the door. "Miss Bradford?" Howie called.

Olivia hurried to throw it open. "Yes?"

The man blinked and stared at her. She laughed and twirled again.

"It's me. Olivia," she murmured.

His lips twitched and she glimpsed his smile. "Yes, ma'am. Mr. Luca is downstairs."

Liv's heart sped up and she nodded. "Do I look okay?"

He swallowed and his face framed into the stern, I'm-a-badass-bodyguard look. Protecting was his job, not handing out compliments. "Yes."

She smirked at Albert when he saw her and reacted just as Howie had. They rode in silence to the lobby. Dominic was pacing back and forth, holding his cellphone to his ear and speaking in low tones when she spotted him. He wore a black suit and black shirt minus a tie. He turned and stopped, his lips ceasing their movement. His gaze found hers and Liv stilled, the world around them dissolving, leaving the two of them in their own little universe.

He undressed her with invisible fingers, removing her clothes piece by piece and enjoying what he discovered. His molten appraisal melted her and left no room for doubt about his intentions or whether or not they were lovers. She was glad she'd allowed the stylist to place sparkly pins in her hair. Her pussy clenched at his hot perusal and he stepped forward. His hand enveloped hers as he brought it to his lips and kissed the back of it.

"You're gorgeous," he croaked.

She beamed a smile at him. "And I'm buzzed," she whispered, giggling. "That champagne was delicious."

"Come on, Olivia. Let's get something in your belly."

"Oh I can think of a couple things I'd like in my belly."

"Behave," he said around a laugh as they stepped out into the night.

Liv halted when she saw the carriage. Dominic didn't give her a chance to speak.

"Come," he said.

Unable to stop herself, she placed a quick kiss on his lips. Once they were settled in, with Dominic seated right next to her and not a space separating where their thighs touched, the driver started the horse off and guided them through the Charleston night, pointing out landmarks.

When they arrived at the restaurant and walked in, another surprise awaited Liv. It was completely empty, filled to the brim with candles and flowers and a row of wait staff.

Dominic captivated and awed her throughout their meal, which started with a round of mint juleps and progressed to she-crab soup, oyster pie, and creamy rice pudding as dessert. When hot buttered rum was brought out, Liv shook her head.

"Oh, no, I can't. I've never drank so much in my life."

It wasn't long after they completed the drink that they left.

Rarely did Dominic roll out one of his cars to drive anyone around. On weekends, he drove one of the sports cars he owned but he was usually alone. It was his thinking time, the time he took to figure out a business problem. Of course, Preston had seen his cars. Well most of them. Dominic hadn't gotten around to showing off his new Ferrari 458 Italia. She was a five-hundred-seventy horsepower, seven-speed beauty. The black grille, red exterior, door handles and front and rear bumpers—as well as the body side moldings— embellished her sleek loveliness to sinful temptation.

He wanted to show Olivia the car and drive her back to his estate where he would present to her the items she'd left behind and he'd sent Albert to purchase. It was sexy and gorgeous, like she was. Getting the car to him while they dined had been a small problem since no one ever drove his cars. Yet, to get it here, he'd had to have Albert and Howie return to the island, retrieve the car and drive it to the restaurant.

He trusted Albert with his life. That car was a different story. It lured a man to test its limits and floor the accelerator. It made him think of sex, power and passion. However when he and Olivia departed the restaurant, he found his car parked out front, with not one scratch. Albert and Howie waited in the Escalade directly behind it.

Howie met him at the car and held out the key.

"Thank you," Dominic murmured, watching Olivia's eyes widen before she screwed her face into nonchalance.

He kissed her on her forehead. Without prompting, she reciprocated, kissing him on his cheek and gracing him with one of her megawatt smiles. He noted Howie's smile and reminded himself to talk to the man. Yes, Olivia was gorgeous and charming and alluring, but she was also off-limits. Just because she was Dominic's captive didn't mean she was fair game.

Captive or not, she was *Dominic's.*

The man reached to open Olivia's door.

"That'll be all for the evening," Dominic warned, removing the man's hand and opening Olivia's door himself.

"Yes, sir."

"Dominic, please," Olivia scolded, rolling her eyes. "You sound like a jealous boyfriend. Howie's only doing his job."

Dominic narrowed his eyes at the bodyguard who kept a straight face. "Good night, Howard."

"Sir." The man rushed away and climbed into the waiting Escalade.

A moment later, Albert steered the SUV away.

Dominic grabbed Olivia and pushed her against the car, sweeping his mouth over hers and kissing her with fierce possessiveness. He placed a thigh between her legs and the heat from her caused his dick to tent his pants. He shifted and rode her high against him, her short skirt no barrier to him.

Measure for measure, she kissed him back, throwing her head back and giving him access to her neck. She rolled against his thigh and moaned, the scent of her desire seeping from her and engorging his cock.

"I'm going to come on you, in you, all over you," he growled, suckling the tender skin of her neck.

"Yeah," she whimpered. "Please."

He pushed against her hard but then stopped, leaving her unsated and wanting.

"Get in." He pushed her trembling body aside and opened the door, shoving her inside. He didn't waste time in getting in and starting the engine. The car purred to life, pure sin to match his wicked mood.

Liv's body still shook as Dominic sped away from the restaurant. She was ready for him now and didn't want to wait the forty-five minutes it would take to get to his house.

He'd gotten her so hot and worked up she couldn't stand it. She remembered reading something in one of her books suggesting naughty places to make love. One was in the car as your man drove. It further instructed the lady to massage her own clit and try to work herself to achieve orgasm at the same time as her lover.

She kicked her shoes off then wiggled her toes before unbuckling her seatbelt and removing her panties.

"What are you doing?"

She leaned across the console, burying her head against his hard thigh.

"Preparing to give you a blowjob while you're driving."

Her body bounced when he swerved but the abrupt maneuver didn't deter her.

"Olivia…" His voice was half warning, half plea.

"I read about it," she explained, trying to loosen his belt. But with his seatbelt on, it was difficult. She unzipped his pants and pulled out his cock.

"It's so thick and beautiful."

She breathed in the earthy smell of him and her clit throbbed. She dragged her tongue across the tip, fascinated by his different textures. The smooth head and ridges of veins and taut skin. She guided him into her mouth, bobbing her head up and down, his grunts and curses urging her on. Her mouth made smacking and slurping sounds, matching Dominic's heavy breathing. Every now and then, she felt the car swerve and Dominic's arms tauten when he rested his elbow lightly on her head to get control of himself.

She gentled her sucks, though. She didn't want his erratic driving to draw the attention of a police officer. Or worse, cause them to crash. Then, when he got control of himself again, she tortured him by suckling his head, licking away the pre-cum and drawing on him hard.

"Fuck! *Olivia!*" he howled, his seed gushing into her mouth in a hot, harsh torrent.

He thrust up his hips and she remembered to relax her throat, just as she'd read, enabling her to take him deeper and suck every last drop he offered to her.

Liv rested her head against his stomach, breathing rapidly. Her lips felt swollen. Dominic pulled to the side of the road, his head thrown back, his grip on the steering wheel so tight his knuckles were turning white. She clutched her seat, determined not to touch herself until he started off again. She had no idea why she wanted to torture him, except perhaps because of the small memory of reading in one of the books how men were aroused and stimulated by visual as much as by sex. She wanted Dominic to feel as overwhelmed by his desire for her as she was for him and she knew if she started touching herself now, he'd take over.

"You sucked my cock for half an hour."

His voice was rough and Liv's nipples tightened. "You fucked my mouth for half an hour."

"Fuck." The tires screeched as he sped away.

The moment he did, Liv reclined back and rested her feet on either side of the seat. She licked her lips, her fingers brushing against her pubic hair. She wondered what he thought of her playing with her pussy. She wasn't bare, though she kept her bush neat. But maybe she should shave. She could just imagine the sensations of his mouth on her if there wasn't hair in the way of his tongue.

She groaned at the thought and arched her hips against her hand.

"Stop."

Dominic's voice reached her through a haze and she groaned again.

"No," she mewled, rolling against her fingers, circling her juices around her tight bud.

"I said to stop."

"Uh-uh. I'm such a bad girl. I think I deserve a spanking." She twisted in her seat, massaging herself, her orgasm spreading through her limbs just as Dominic stopped in his driveway. The front porch was well lit and sprawling.

Liv blinked as her door was yanked open and she was pulled out. He lifted her into his arms, pinning her against the car and ramming into her. She screamed, coming around him a moment before he spurted into her. His cock still buried inside her, he plunged his tongue into her mouth, his eyes glittering, his hands fisting in her hair and ruining the lovely style. Abruptly he pulled out of her and let her fall to her feet. The pavement was cool, the air a sultry breeze against her flushed skin.

After some moments, he took her hand and led her through the door and into the foyer. The house was silent and she wondered where everyone was. The soles of his shoes clipped over the marble, her bare feet soundless.

Once they reached his bedroom, he said, "Undress."

The harsh command in his voice weakened Liv's knees. Her fingers trembled as she tried to unfasten the buttons. He made an impatient sound and reached for her.

"No. Please don't tear it. This is the finest thing I've ever had."

His frustration evident, he undid her buttons, taking care not to tear either the shirt or the skirt before he unhooked her bra.

Grasping her waist, Dominic lifted her then deposited her on his bed. She saw her bag at the foot.

"Lie flat, Olivia," he demanded in a commanding tone.

Excitement raced through her at being so completely at Dominic's mercy. She lay on her back and heard the jingle of her handcuffs, anticipating the moment he fastened each arm to the headboard. Instead he handcuffed her as though she were a prisoner and then used the other pair to fasten her to the bed. Before he started on her feet, he tied the blindfold around her eyes. Liv listened for his movements, surprised how attuned her other senses became when she didn't have sight.

Something soft tickled her calf and then she felt the sash around her left ankle. He repeated the process, tying her right ankle. His fingers slid across her belly, circled the globes of her breasts before tweaking her nipples.

She groaned.

"Not a sound," he purred.

Her breath hitched and she bit down on her lip.

Movement. Fluttery touches. Sheets rustling. His heat surrounded her as he straddled her thighs. The heaviness of his erection settled against her belly, his balls against her mound. Fingers squeezed one of her achy nipples and she strained against her restraints. He slid down her legs, keeping most of his weight off her, his cock massaging her clit before sliding down her seam. He poised at the entrance of her sex, pushed the wide head inside.

Liv moaned again, attempting to impale herself on him. He growled and removed his cock. A light slap on her sex followed and she moaned again.

"No." Another light smack against her mons punctuated that word, repeated when he added the next word. "Talking. Not a sound." With each word he tapped her sensitive flesh.

Her womb was tight, her sex wetter than it had ever been before. She was on the verge of coming. Fainting. Dying.

He leaned over and bit her nipple and she shook.

"Don't you dare come."

He slid his length against her bud and she trembled again, her legs shaking as if her body was deprived of heat. To the contrary, she was burning from the inside out. Dominic was killing her in slow degrees.

"We almost wrecked because of your games."

She wasn't going to last. She knew it. Either she was going to have an orgasm or she would beg him to take her.

"You like sucking my dick?"

Her breaths came in short pants. From somewhere deep inside her, she felt a swell of moisture, a great frenzy of excitement that sent her closer and closer to her orgasm. "Y-yes."

He used his cock to hit her clit over and over, her center hot and pulsing, and she couldn't stop it, couldn't prevent the rush of wetness, her scream of exultation and satisfaction. He rose above her, his cock against her lips. She tried to rise and take him in her mouth but she was weak and sated from her orgasm. A moment later, she felt his seed dripping down her lips and chin.

"I told you not to come."

He unfastened her ankles and she moved her legs restlessly. Her body needed to be filled with his hard flesh. She tried to think of how many times he'd come, tried to remember the maximum amount of times a man could come. But he was unfastening the cuff from the headboard and turning her over onto her belly before restraining her to the bed again.

"I believe you asked for a spanking."

Her mind searched for the conversation, the anticipation of what he would do next drying her mouth. Her breasts pushed against his silk sheets, her nipples hurting and sensitive. He caressed her ass then cracked his palm against it, a hard, rounded hit that made her eyes sting behind the mask.

He slapped her again and a ragged cry tore from her lips, caught between pain and pleasure. He hit her a final time before ceasing.

A cold liquid slid between her ass cheeks. Sensation raced through her as hard rubber vibrated against her clit. He pulled her ass in the air and she whimpered, rolling her hips in invitation. His growl sent of rush of wetness to her pussy. At the moist heat of his tongue between her legs, she trembled. Too soon, he pulled away and she surged back searching for the pleasure of his mouth and crying out in frustration when her ass met air and her restraints halted her. Her arms ached, stretched above her head, but she ignored the discomfort to submit to Dominic. That's what he wanted. More importantly, that's what she wanted and he knew it. Her head and breasts were pushed against the bed. He swirled the flavored lubricant around her tight little hole, replacing his fingers with his mouth while the vibrator pulsed against her nub. His tongue circled her backdoor, the lubricant mingling with his saliva and heating.

She sucked in air, her head spinning, her senses careening together, overloaded, overwhelmed. Her cries alternated between screams and pleas and she barely recognized them as her own. Her pussy was clenching and unclenching around the dildo, the in and out motion, the sharp pulses almost painful now.

She didn't know what to do or say to make him end this torture. Every time she reached the breaking point, he gentled his tongue and the toy. He wasn't letting her come and he wasn't stopping. Frantic, she moaned like an animal in pain, a sob breaking through.

He decided to show her a little mercy and halted. She wanted to come but she was afraid he'd start his sensual assault again and still deny her orgasm. Suddenly her wrists were free and she brought them to her sides, limp, exhausted, throbbing. Next, he untied her feet and removed her blindfold. She rolled onto her back.

His image blurred in front of her until she readjusted to the soft lighting. They stared at one another for long moments and his nostrils flared. He kissed his way down her body before stretching her legs wide. He sniffed her entire seam, opened her pussy lips and smelled her again.

"So fucking good." In a slow, tortuous lick, he dragged his tongue across her clit.

Liv gripped his hair and pushed against his mouth, holding him there.

"Faster!" she screamed. "Harder!"

Just in case he didn't understand, she gyrated against his mouth, spreading her legs wider.

"Eat all of me!" she cried. "Lick my pussy."

Her words unleashed something inside him. His mouth covered her sex and sucked her bud. His licks became fast, barely there, before turning brutal and unrelenting. She refused to let go of his head, afraid he would stop, afraid he would deny her again.

If he did, she *would* die. He shoved two fingers into her and electricity flashed through her nerve endings. She felt the sensation of his fingering from the tips of her nipples and deep down into her core. Her grip relaxed on his head and she spiraled into mindless screams and ecstasy, twisting against his mouth, her hips rising high in the air. This time though, he didn't release her. He anticipated her moves and twisted and rose with her, using his mouth as a lethal weapon. His fingers tugged and hooked inside her, finding a spot he'd never touched before and her juices gushed from her.

His mouth slowed against her and he pulled his fingers out of her. He rose above her, resting his weight on his knees and elbows, staring into her eyes.

Something had happened to her tonight. No, today. She wanted to stay with him, discover more about him. She was afraid she'd grown attached to him, afraid he'd leave an awful void when he returned her to Blaine. She wanted to ask him to let her stay. But no. If he felt they had a chance at a relationship, she wouldn't have to ask.

Her lower lip trembled. His look softened and she thought he might say something. Instead he sank into her and rested his chin atop the crown of her head. This time, though, instead of their wild sex, he made love to her. Their rough sex had been an outlet for their attraction and expelled frustration. Tonight, though, Dominic's tenderness made her believe he thought more of her than just as a bargaining chip with Blaine. She couldn't have been more grateful that he'd treated her as if she were important.

The next morning, she awakened before Dominic, finding her leg draped over his body, her head in the crook of his arm. His hard dick pressed against his thigh and she rubbed her pussy against his hip, wishing he was inside of her. The realization that their time together was coming to an end intruded on her desire and she pulled away from him to stare at the ceiling, her mind running a million miles a minute. Most of her thoughts centered around Dominic and finding a way to stay with him. But he'd already told her how he felt about the prospect of a future between them. There was none.

Undoubtedly, he was right. For them to have had anything more, she would need to tell him that *she'd* been the one to break into his system. Without her help, Blaine never would've bested Dominic. Her actions sent equal parts shame and guilt through her. Dominic would never understand why she'd gone along with Blaine's wild schemes.

The change in Dominic's breathing alerted Liv he'd awakened. Not wanting to ruin the silence between them, Liv kept quiet.

Sighing, he drew her back into his arms and tangled a hand in her hair. She hummed low in her throat when he began caressing her scalp.

"The asshole called," he announced, dousing the desire rising in her at his touch.

She'd known all along they would go their separate ways. Since she couldn't remember ever being associated with anyone for a very long time, with the exception of her mother and brother, she didn't know why she felt so lost at the prospect of never seeing Dominic again.

"Did you hear me, Olivia?"

"Yes," she whispered, thinking maybe she should skim her fingertips across the wide expanse of his chest. Or kiss him. Or rise up, straddle him, and sink her pussy onto his hard cock. But she didn't do either. His words kept her still, as did the fact that he seemed unperturbed by their imminent separation.

"I have a meeting at the office and a couple of things to see to," he went on. "We'll fly out this afternoon."

She swallowed, hating the burn in her eyes indicating she was on the verge of tears. But if there was ever anyone she wanted to keep in her life, it was Dominic. She wanted to know everything about him. He made her laugh. He made her angry and jealous. And he was teaching her about pleasure.

The thought of never seeing him again...What was she thinking? Her duplicity damaged any future they might've had. He might never know she'd assisted Blaine. Then again, he could discover how she'd hacked into his company next week. She could've even told him this morning, when he'd been in a strange mood and had flattened his large hand against her belly.

"You could be pregnant," he said when she couldn't find words to offer.

No, she couldn't be since she was on The Pill, but the subject of birth control had never come up between them. *Fuckity-fuck.* It hit her that she hadn't taken the contraceptive in two days. The day of her kidnapping she'd taken it, though, so that hopefully accounted to protect her.

He slipped his fingers through her hair. "You have your entire life ahead of you. A child would tie you down."

He traced her lips, her nose, and her jaw as if he wanted to memorize her features. Hurt at the latest loss facing her, she didn't want Dominic's touch to affect her, so she heaved in a breath and told him the truth. "Never. It would give me something to love. I never tied my momma down." At least, she hoped she hadn't.

She frowned to hide her growing despair. No matter how many times she repeated her mantra of *no regrets and no running*, she couldn't seem to feel the same sense of carelessness the sentiment brought about. After living by it for so many months, she should've latched onto it easily now.

"Will you let me know if you've conceived?"

He was withdrawing from her, the tone of his voice and the way he watched her changing from passionate to kind.

"Would you want to know?"

"Of course. That would be my child."

"I'm on The Pill."

He stared at her in silence for long moments. "If I haven't missed my guess, and I rarely do, you haven't taken them while you've been my guest."

Dominic seemed to read her so well, better than anyone she'd ever met. Despite everything, he actually took the time to pay attention to her. "Guest, huh?" she echoed, a small smile tipping her lips.

His answering grin softened the hard beauty of his face.

"You don't smile enough," she said softly, changing the subject of contraception and babies. She was too discombobulated over leaving Dominic to worry about a pregnancy that would have her mother's life replay through Liv's mistakes.

"I'm not a smiler," he confided.

"No shit," she retorted with a giggle, making little whirly motions on his chest.

He cleared his throat. "You make me smile. I like you, Olivia."

At his admission, she lifted up on her elbow, almost afraid to hear the rest of whatever he had to say. Many people had *liked* her. They'd still been only walks-ons in her life. Nothing permanent, just temporary fillers.

"When I return you to fuckhead, I'd like us to keep in touch."

"Truly?" she whispered, before her thoughts intruded and dampened her lifting spirits. "What about your girlfriend?" And Liv's hacking?

"I already told you Felicia wasn't truly my girlfriend. Besides, whatever she might've been is no more. She resigned yesterday."

"Why?"

"She wanted me to forego my plans with you. I refused."

"And that's it? Once I'm gone, she'll come back." Why was she making a big deal out of this when she had secrets of her own? "I overheard Albert and Howie speculating that I'd leave sooner than the three days because Felicia wouldn't be happy."

He narrowed his eyes. "Is that so?" he asked coolly.

"I wasn't eavesdropping," she began defensively, though that's exactly what she'd been doing.

"It doesn't matter if you were or not," he barked. "I intend to talk to them. If they value their positions, they'll not discuss my goddamn personal business."

"Howie was just agreeing to what Albert was saying."

"You seem inordinately fond of Howie."

Olivia rolled her eyes at his frosty words. Until it dawned on her. He was jealous, as she'd been about Felicia. "I think Albert's a sneaky weasel," she responded, almost giddy at the thought of Dominic being jealous over her. "Which may come across as having an inordinate fondness for Howie."

"Albert is rather stern," he agreed. "But I happen to trust him."

"Good for you. I still think he's an asshole."

"We'll discuss my protection officers at a later date," he rumbled, grabbing her wrist and tugging her toward him. He kissed her lips. No tongue-play was involved, but it still made her want to fuck his brains out. "I've already put my phone number in your phone and vice versa. Can we try to put our inauspicious beginning behind us and get to know one another?"

"Yes, Dominic," she said, almost confessing then and there, but so afraid he'd never want anything to do with her ever again.

Looking pleased, he got out of bed, his erection bobbing as he walked toward the bathroom. The sight of his hard cock, so needy and ready, sent hot longing through Liv.

He smirked at her. "Care to join me in the shower?"

She laughed and hurried to him, knowing she'd never look at a shower the same way by the time Dominic finished with her.

Before leaving for the day, he had given her gift bags containing every item she'd left behind at all the stores.

Yet, when they headed to the airport later that evening, the things remained in Charleston. She'd purposely left them behind. In good conscience, Liv couldn't take the clothes, lingerie and shoes, not when she was so overcome with guilt.

CHAPTER SEVEN

The first time Olivia met her half-brother, she'd been five and he'd been twenty. He'd awed her because he'd been all height and brawn with black hair and green eyes that matched hers. She'd only seen men who looked like Blaine on television and in magazines. Their father had been handsome too, but there'd been a presence about Blaine. She hadn't yet realized the aura surrounding him had bits of insanity and a whole lot of ruthlessness included. He'd still been nice. Or as nice as Blaine had ever been to her. He'd called her Miss Hopkins because their father hadn't yet acknowledged her as a Bradford. Every now and then, he'd slipped in "squirt" and "brat". But the way he'd said it hadn't hurt Olivia's feelings. To the contrary, his teasing tone had made her giggle. From the moment he'd heard her mother call her "Livvie" that had been Blaine's name for her as well.

By the age of ten, she'd become a Bradford. Their father's wife—Blaine's lauded mother—had died so their father recognized Olivia as his offspring. That was the turning point in her and Blaine's relationship. He'd changed, become a complete sonofabitch to her. By the time she was fifteen their father had died. Though he'd recognized her in life, in death he'd forgotten about her, not even leaving her a wallet-sized photo of himself.

Her mother had been crushed and Blaine had been smug.

An attitude that infused him now as he eyed her standing next to Dominic in the middle of Blaine's spacious office. Albert and Howie flanked her and Dominic, their 9mms as visible as the ones her brother's security guys had. The undercurrent of dislike threatened to erupt into violence at any moment.

Blaine strolled around to his desk, a gilt and marble monstrosity he'd inherited from their father. He slid a suitcase to the edge. Dominic sauntered forward and snapped open the locks. Olivia strained her neck to see the contents. Her eyes bulged at the stacks of one hundred dollar bills inside. Dominic lifted the top row and then the second and then the third.

"It's all here." Dominic reclosed and secured the suitcase with efficiency.

"As promised," Blaine said in bored tones. He studied his manicured hands. "Now if you don't mind, please return my sister to me."

Dominic nodded to Albert, ignoring her as he brushed past her. She willed him to acknowledge her, to tell her goodbye. Anything. Instead he spoke to Howie in low tones as Albert escorted her to Blaine. Her brother shoved her toward his meanest bodyguard, the one she hated with everything in her. She called him Ape, refusing to remember his name. She'd spit in his face but she'd never call him by name.

"Take her," Blaine ordered in a loud whisper and he winked at the big, blond Neanderthal.

Liv flinched. She and Blaine's men heard, but Dominic, Albert and Howie hadn't. She didn't like the connotations in her brother's words. She liked even less the wicked grin Ape gave her. She didn't want Dominic to help her. He wanted to explore their attraction and she couldn't destroy that now. Instead of involving him and giving Blaine ammunition to hurt her, she'd run in the opposite direction as soon as she got outside the building.

"We both have what we wanted, Luca," Blaine called. "I'll thank you to leave my office."

Ape began to march Liv toward the door. He'd never had much sense, blindly following Blaine's orders. Grunted a few words. Grunted down his meals. Just *grunted*.

If he thought she would go with him and allow him to do whatever he intended to do to her, he was more of an idiot than she'd thought. Damn Blaine. She didn't need him.

Dominic stopped talking, obviously arrested by Ape's progression with her. He moved away from Albert and Howie, creating the opening Liv needed to scoot through. Her survival instincts kicked in, the ones she'd used before she'd met Dominic, where she only knew how to run and regroup. Ape yanked her and Liv swung, catching him in the nose before she turned and kneed him in the groin for good measure.

"Livvie!"

"Olivia!"

She didn't stop to acknowledge her brother's and Dominic's calls. She shot through the opening Dominic had created and ran toward the emergency stairwell. She had twenty flights until she reached the ground and by then they would've taken the elevator to get her.

Like hell.

The recent fire inspection of the building ran through her mind. The elevators would descend to the lobby and remain open until the alarm was cleared. She paused for a brief second then yanked down the handle on the fire alarm. The loud whirring drowned out the hell breaking loose in Blaine's office. Water rained down, drenching the reception area.

Not her problem, even though she was soaked too. The elevators would be disabled, the most important thing. She ran down the first flight of stairs, almost tumbling head over heels at the sound of footsteps behind her.

"Olivia!"

"Livvie, stop right now, damn you."

Blaine was as idiotic as Ape if he believed she was going to stop.

Eighteen more flights. A cramp seized her side and she cursed. But she refused to halt. She'd have to be disabled before she gave in.

"Olivia!"

Dominic. But she wasn't even going to stop for him. He'd just desert her and decide to send her back to Blaine after their wonderful time together and their conversation from yesterday. Early on, he'd said a relationship with her was out of the question. This would be the fuel he needed to stick to that.

"I already know you fucked him, Livvie."

And? How was *that* supposed to matter in the great scheme of things? Asshole for a brother. Overgrown Ape intent upon assault with asshole brother's blessings. Lost virginity as payment for asshole brother's crimes.

"Would you shut the fuck up, you asshole?"

Dominic again. She would've laughed if she hadn't been in such a hurry and if she could catch her breath.

What floor was she on? God. Only sixteen. She realized the whir of the alarm had stopped and wondered what would happen next. Water dripped from Liv, made her clothes cling to her.

"You have a very thorough assistant, Luca," Blaine yelled.

He didn't have to shout so loud. Liv knew he did so because he wanted her to hear. But they were in a closed stairwell, late at night, with only the sound of her harsh breathing and their pounding footsteps. She couldn't help but hear.

"She told me you decided to send Livvie home after Felicia pointed out she was ready to spit out your kid. Ready to become Mrs. Dominic Luca."

Liv stumbled at that, nearly losing her balance. He'd told her something different yesterday and...*Stop, Liv. Blaine's a manipulating asshole.* She had more reason to believe what Dominic said over Blaine's words.

She hobbled a step. The cramp in her side traveled to her thigh and she had to halt on the landing of the thirteenth floor. Dominic stood three steps above her, her brother four steps above him. She realized other men were coming to a halt too. The bodyguards must've followed their bosses.

"Felicia told me you fucked Olivia as retribution. You've gotten your revenge, Dominic," Blaine continued. "As well as your money."

A distressed cry escaped Liv. Despite her reasoning about Blaine's morals, she couldn't deny the surge of hurt at his triumphant words. It was bad enough *she* knew the reason he'd had sex with her. To tell his girlfriend, ex or not... Liv couldn't bear the thought. The sob that escaped her bounced off the walls and she couldn't seem to stop the tears of anger and anguish. Dominic and Felicia must've shared a good laugh over her.

Blaine stepped around Dominic and closed the distance between them. He clamped his hand on her shoulder, his grip tight and brutal. "I don't need you to turn into a female on me now."

What the fuck? "I've always been a girl, jerkwad," she growled in frustration. "You just chose to see me as an object. A robot to order around, so I'm not sure how you've suddenly opened your eyes and—"

Blaine indicated her tears. "Crying, Livvie," he interrupted with impatience. "You don't cry. You don't coo. You don't giggle. You drive fast. You laugh loud. And you fight like a pro." He shook her. "So man the fuck up now, suck up your tears and face the goddamn music."

He shoved her toward the steps. She grabbed the railing in the nick of time. *Fight, Liv.* That's what Blaine expected of her. But she was so tired, physically exhausted and emotionally battered. Dominic charged behind Blaine, swung the door open to the level they were on and shoved him through it. The sound of flesh meeting flesh gratified her. Howie, Ape and the rest of her brother's bodyguards rushed forward. It was their job to get killed on behalf of their bosses. They couldn't allow those bosses to murder each other.

Liv turned, her legs shaky, determination to reach the bottom floor filling her with resolve.

"Stop, Luca! Stop!" Blaine pleaded, slowing Liv's steps.

She paused, jumping at her brother's agony-filled scream.

"My nose. You've broken my goddamn nose."

A body banged against the door and it opened. A sliver of light shafted into the stairwell and Liv crept down two more steps.

"It was Livvie," Blaine whined. "I couldn't have gotten those damn files if she hadn't hacked into your company's system."

"You're a goddamn liar. Olivia had nothing to do with it."

She cringed, shrinking against the wall, unable to move at Dominic's staunch defense of her.

"She lied to you about her age, didn't she? Told you she was twenty-five when she was twenty-one."

The door flew open, slamming against the concrete wall so hard Liv feared it had been cracked. No, this wasn't happening. Her world wasn't crashing around her. But it was and there'd be no turning back. Dominic stood on the landing, his eyes burning with fury. His gaze fell to her. Something in her features must've given away her guilt. The guilt was so much worse than her pain over Dominic's discovery. She'd never forget the exact moment he realized what she'd done.

She'd never seen that type of rage contorting a man's face in her entire life.

Dominic stared at Olivia, seeing the truth of Blaine's words in her huge eyes and pale face. All along he'd had the enemy in his house. In his bed. In his head.

He glowered at her, took a step forward, unsure of what he intended to do. He couldn't believe her duplicity. After he'd been lured in by her, so much so that he thought a relationship with her possible. In a haze of fury and betrayal, he reached her. Instead of running as a sane person would do, she stared at him.

"Why?" His voice was soft, lethal, and he restrained himself from grabbing her.

"Let me explain," she began.

"Explain?" Dominic's laughter was cold. "Explain how you allowed me to implicate your brother when you were as guilty as he was? Or explain how I allowed you to play me? What would you like to explain?"

"My situation," she shouted. "My desperation."

Anger blinded him and he did grab her and shake her. "Bullshit. There's not a desperate bone in your body. You're full of deceit and duplicity."

Her breasts rose and fell as she puffed out short bursts of air. Color suffused her cheeks. She glanced over his shoulder and Dominic followed the direction of her gaze. Blaine stood behind Dominic, her brother's face and eyes swelling, nose still bleeding.

"If that's what you believe, just go," Olivia cried, jerking herself out of his grasp and grabbing hold of the steel banister just in time to prevent herself from careening down the stairs. "Go. I don't need you. I don't need anyone."

With one final look at him, she turned and continued down the staircase, slower now since no one gave chase. Dominic was too angry to stop her. Weary, he brushed past Blaine and stepped into the deserted corridor of the fifteenth floor. He shoved his hands through his hair, trying to control his temper.

"I'll thank you to leave my building," Blaine said.

His bored tone snapped Dominic's control and he turned and slammed his fist in the man's face again. "In case you've forgotten, I own part of this company." He picked Blaine up by the lapels and whacked him again. "It wasn't enough I was saving your sorry family from ruin, was it? Or was this Olivia's idea?"

"Livvie?" he slurred. "The only thing Livvie ever wanted was an easier life for her mother and a college degree."

The huge bodyguard who'd attempted to paw Olivia shoved a chair toward Blaine. Dominic released Bradford. He dropped into the chair and leaned his head back, pulling his red handkerchief from his front pocket.

"I beg your pardon?"

"You heard me, damn it, Luca." Blaine sighed. "Dad only sent Olivia a new laptop every year whenever Connie—her mother—forwarded a new address. They never stayed in one place for long."

Dominic started for Blaine and the giant bodyguard stepped between them.

"Move," Dominic ordered the man.

The fool just shook his head.

Dominic crashed a backhanded fist into the big man's jaw before elbowing him in the nose, gratified at his scream. He'd wanted to do that since the man had put his hands on Olivia.

"Get him out of here," Dominic ordered the other men.

They looked to Blaine, and Dominic growled an obscenity that obviously convinced them he was in charge for the moment. Howie lurked in the shadows and Dominic gestured for him.

"Find some ice for Bradford."

Blaine grimaced. "A doctor would be better."

"You get to suffer a few moments," Dominic returned without remorse as Howie departed via the stairwell.

Dominic wondered if Olivia had made it to the ground floor yet. As if he cared. He'd deal with her once he finished with her asshole of a brother.

"You had to know your actions would be traced. You have to be brilliant not to have your hacking discovered," Dominic told Bradford.

"That's what Livvie said," Blaine admitted. "I needed the money I'd make off the information in those files. Sue me! Livvie is damn good with computers. It was her escape. She can figure out LINUX and all sorts of code."

A muscle pulsed in Dominic's jaw. He couldn't understand why he felt her betrayal so keenly. Worse, why did he want to try to understand her actions? It shouldn't have mattered. She was his enemy now and she had to be dealt with. "Using her skills, the two of you intended to bleed me dry?"

"No! I swear. It wasn't like that. I told you I would give you money when I released the plans. I was going to take the credit for the idea."

"You're a fucking asshole."

Blaine raised his head to glare out of the eye not swollen shut.

"Enough about Olivia." She'd been vulnerable to her brother because she wanted to go to college. Wasn't she? Or was Dominic merely justifying her behavior. His hadn't been much better. Had it? He hadn't known she'd been involved and he'd kidnapped her. In a way, it was almost a relief to discover she'd played a role. He froze. He was very good at justifying his ruthlessness, which was what he was doing now. He'd once heard that two wrongs didn't make a right and he'd definitely wronged Olivia first for the simple reason he'd had no clue about her activities. Fuck, this was all so complicated in his head. Relationships weren't his specialty, so he wasn't sure if his need to hear Olivia out and let her explain, offer his own apology to her, was right. However, he knew how to conduct business, so he refocused on Blaine who'd kept his attention on Dominic. "You had to have had inside help to crack into my computer system. Who assisted you? Felicia? Preston? Who?"

Darting his eyes away, Blaine blew out a breath. "Neither."

Dominic narrowed his eyes, giving the other man to the count of three.

"It was Albert."

The words came like a blow to Dominic and he reeled back, unable to do anything more than blink. Albert? "My bodyguard?"

One terse nod served as the answer.

"Did Olivia know that?"

"No. Livvie didn't know who my contact was."

Dominic paused and looked around, going through the events of the past half hour in his head. The last time he'd seen Albert, the man had been standing upstairs in Blaine's office, holding the suitcase full of money. In all the scuffling since, Dominic didn't remember glimpsing Albert once.

Olivia ran across his mind. The hurt in her eyes when he'd pushed her away after she'd asked him to let her explain. Her defiance when she'd shouted she didn't need anyone. Her complete dislike of Albert...

Dominic sucked in a breath and pulled out his cell phone. Not bothering to explain to Blaine, he headed toward the stairwell, hoping his instincts were wrong.

Hoping Olivia hadn't fallen into the bodyguard's clutches.

Liv covered her ears to drown out the sound of the sirens, taking in deep gulps of air. Exhaustion threatened to bring her to her knees so she leaned against the smooth stone of the building. She refused to cry and feel sorry for herself. She'd known Dominic would be furious if he discovered her role in this entire affair.

She needed to get to Karen's house and ask if she could stay there for a few days. Otherwise, she'd be on the streets and—

The barrel of a gun jammed into her forehead and she raised her gaze to the unfriendly face of Dominic's bodyguard, Albert, inches from hers.

"Any funny moves and you're dead," he warned. "Come with me and walk as if nothing is wrong."

He put his arm around her as if holding her in a lover's embrace. The gun pressed into her side and without a word, Liv suppressed a shudder. Albert didn't like her and she'd always gotten the creeps from him, sensing he wouldn't hesitate to cross the line into lawless activities. She wasn't sure who was the bigger asshole—Blaine, who apparently had no qualms about turning her over to his bodyguards, or Dominic, who wanted her dead.

One might argue that it was possible to recover from forced sex but death was permanent. Neither appealed to Liv. It was hard for her to process that Dominic sent his bodyguard after her to kill her. She didn't think what she'd done warranted her life to make amends. Though she knew what she'd done at Blaine's directive was both wrong and illegal, she hadn't realized how much her ambition and the prospect of the Bradford money paying her way through college blinded her to morality. She'd acquired the same sense of entitlement Blaine had, and her actions shamed her.

"Smile," Albert commanded in a whisper. "Can't have people thinking something's not right. Like maybe you're being kidnapped or something."

Kidnapped? No, not again. She laughed at the irony. "That's me. Whenever you have to kidnap someone..." She pointed to herself.

"Don't overdo it. Too much happy can also draw unwanted attention." He jiggled the pistol against her side. "This pistol has a hair trigger."

Liv flinched, aware he wanted to frighten her by speaking the ominous words. "Duly noted. Where are you taking me?"

"Around this corner we're coming up on, I have a rented sedan."

A moment later, Olivia found herself at the driver's side door of a newer model Toyota. Albert unlocked the doors with the remote keyless entry fob and transferred the gun to the back of Liv's head.

"Get in."

That was the absolute last thing she wanted to do because her chances of survival would decrease substantially. She mightn't have learned much in Tai Chi but she knew it was less about resisting and more about yielding to the attack so she could focus all her energy in her self-defense movements and redirect the violence toward the perpetrator.

Albert pressed her against the car, pinning her body to the warm metal. "Get in," he repeated.

The single whip technique called for a shoulder strike to the opponent's ribs, an elbow hit to the torso, finger jabs to the throat or eyes. She wiggled, trying to separate herself from Albert.

"Try anything and I shoot."

Liv gritted her teeth, her brain sifting through endless possibilities. "What do you expect me to do?"

"Get in."

Besides that, she thought with frustration and aggravation. *Yield, Liv.* She'd get in, lull him into believing she was cooperating. She thought about running in the time it took him to walk around the front bumper and slide next to her in the passenger seat, but she didn't trust Albert not to fire.

"Start the goddamn car and drive the fuck off," Albert yelled, the gun now at her temple.

He turned the key and the motor revved to life. He slid his foot over to the accelerator and pressed down hard. With one hand on the gun and the other on the steering wheel, he sped away from the curb, barely avoiding oncoming traffic. Liv screamed and covered her eyes, preparing herself for impact. It never came.

"Take the fucking wheel," he snarled.

She gripped the wheel with both hands, the car weaving. "I don't know how to drive!"

Albert maneuvered the car onto a deserted side street and pulled to a stop. He stared at her as though he were trying to decide his next move. "Fuck! I'll drive. Slide over to this side, you little idiot."

He stepped out and slammed the passenger-side door, starting around the automobile to get to the driver's side. She didn't want to kill the man, so the moment he cleared the path of the car, Olivia floored the accelerator, propelling the car to a high rate of speed in a few seconds. She prayed Albert realized gunfire might draw attention and decided against taking aim at her. Then again, he might be so pissed off that she'd lied about not knowing how to drive, he wouldn't care what happened after he fired the gun. The man took pleasure in pleasing Dominic and his latest order to get rid of Olivia was an epic fail.

Liv's heart pounded with fear and she gripped the steering wheel, drawing in deep breaths to calm her racing pulse. It took her a moment to realize Albert hadn't fired and she'd reached the relative safety of Canal Street, a major thoroughfare in the city.

She drove around, heading lake-bound on Canal until she reached Carrollton Avenue and awareness seeped in. She was heading toward Blaine's house, a habit she'd formed from her months of living there.

Sighing, she turned into the parking lot of a grocery store. She wasn't sure she could trust Karen, but as her friend, perhaps, Karen would understand her predicament. Liv drew her phone from the pocket of her jeans and pressed the speed dial for Karen's number.

"Livvie!" Karen answered on the third ring. "Blaine and Dominic Luca have been here looking for you. What did you do? Where are you?"

Karen's voice sounded breathless, almost cautious, so unlike her carefree tone, Liv decided her friend asked the questions for information rather than concern.

"Karen, I...haven't done...um, what did they say?"

"That you'd run away." Karen's silence lasted a heartbeat then she cleared her throat and continued. "Er, I don't think they'll return. Why don't you come here and we can get to the bottom of this."

"Sounds like a plan," Olivia responded, over-bright. Dominic hunting for her would fill Karen with curiosity, even as she offered advice on, and shelter from, everything else.

"Um, Liv?"

"I'm here."

"Um...how long will it take you to get here?"

Liv scowled and tapped her fingers on the steering wheel. "Why?"

"Er, no reason. Just can't wait to see you."

"Right. I'll see you in a bit," she promised, flipping her phone closed, thankful her mother hadn't raised a fool.

Karen was anxious to betray her to those assholes. *Thanks but no thanks.*

Dominic never would've guessed on the flight from Charleston that he would end up in Blaine Bradford's house, worried senseless about Olivia and zeroing in on a trusted bodyguard as the person who'd betrayed him.

And yet here he was, pacing Bradford's study, frowning at Olivia's friend, Karen, who'd just arrived after waiting for Olivia's arrival at her house for over two hours. When Karen realized Olivia wouldn't show, she'd called Blaine and he'd ordered her over. Now Karen sat, tears slipping down her cheeks as she voiced her concern for her friend.

Blaine scowled. "Olivia isn't stupid, Karen. If the conversation you relayed to me is the exact one you had with Livvie, then she would've been suspicious. Your normal nosiness was glaringly absent."

Karen flipped her bone-straight hair over her shoulder and swiped at her eyes. She glared at Blaine. "If you were a better brother, she would've found you. Now she's out there all alone."

"And? Livvie knows how to take care of herself. She's used to being alone. What do you think she did when her mother was out whoring to earn money for food?"

Karen squeaked and her mouth fell open.

"That's right. Not only isn't she rich, but she's my bastard half-sister, whose mother was one of the maids in the household." He shrugged. "She ended up having to turn tricks just to keep Liv fed."

"Shut up, Bradford," Dominic growled. "For the entire night, you've been hell-bent on humiliating Olivia and turning everyone against her."

"I spoke the truth and it worked, didn't it?"

"No," Dominic and Karen chorused.

"You two can't be serious?" Blaine's eyes widened. "Do you know the trouble I went through to convince Garth to walk away from Olivia? I need her with me and if she believes she's all alone in this world, she'll come back."

"To do your hacking?" Dominic said.

"Liv is smart. I told you I didn't mean any harm, Luca. I needed money. Liv got the files I needed. But I realized I misused her talent. She might be able to find a solution and help Bradford Industries out of failing. Legally," he added when Dominic started for him.

"Why did she run in the first place?" Karen unzipped her purse and pulled out a fresh Kleenex. "She was back, able to look forward to starting school. What did you tell her, Blaine?"

The man shoved his hands in his pockets. "I insinuated I would allow, er, Denefew—the one she calls Ape—to..." His voice trailed off.

"Say it," Dominic demanded, Olivia's sudden panic making sense now. Why hadn't he realized?

"I never would've given my sister to him. She's such a damn handful. She just needed a little fear put into her."

A commotion prevented Dominic's response. He watched as Howie and Ape hustled in Albert. Dominic's IT department had been tracking the bodyguard via his cell phone and had called with an approximate location forty-five minutes ago. Dominic knew Olivia's location too. He just wasn't sharing. Before he went to her, however, he needed to deal with Albert.

The bald-headed man glared at Dominic.

"I should've shot her when I had the gun to her head," Albert offered.

Dominic sucked in a breath, the thought of Olivia in danger sending his protective instincts into overdrive. Although he knew where she was, he didn't know her condition. If Albert hurt her... Dominic slammed his fist into the other man's jaw. "What did you do to her?"

Albert shook his head as if he were shaking off Dominic's blow. "Nothing. She got away. Led me to believe she didn't know how to drive. Little bitch. The moment I got out to go to the driver's side, she sped off. I should've shot her anyway. Made me feel like a goddamn fool."

"Again," Howie offered. "I seem to recall she got the best of you two or three times."

Turning halfway, Albert growled.

"Call the police. Howard, come with me." Dominic swung a warning gaze to Bradford. "I trust your men can handle Albert until the authorities arrive?"

Blaine swallowed, blinked. "You...you aren't having me arrested?"

Dominic's jaw clenched. "I'd have to have Olivia arrested as well and that I won't do."

Liv sat on a stone bench in Audubon Park. Soon, dawn would burrow through the pitch darkness and lighten the sky with dusky orange. She'd ditched the car in the empty parking lot of the zoo and used the flashlight app on her cellphone to guide her way from Magazine Street to where she sat now.

Her heart constricted at the thought of Dominic and their time together. But people had always breezed into her life and then traipsed right back out, never to be heard from again.

Footsteps approached and she shrank back into the shadows. A flashlight glared on her and around her, the brightness bouncing off her jeans and hurting her eyes.

"Looking for my dog," a man muttered.

He stopped in front of her and Liv's entire body tensed. He fidgeted, adjusting his position, jiggling coins in his pocket, the light bouncing with his movements. She told herself to remain still and not to raise her head, though she knew it could be anyone and, more than likely, was a random stranger who had really lost his dog.

A pair of headlights shone against the bark of the trees and the carpet of grass. Liv swallowed, on high alert. Dominic would be out searching for her. As would Blaine. She shuddered.

"Have you seen it?" the man persisted, his voice low and indistinguishable. "She's a puggle. You know, part beagle, part pug?"

The headlights died away. Liv thought about pretending to be asleep but debated the wisdom. If he thought her so vulnerable, he might accost her. If she didn't answer, he would just continue to stand there with his bright light.

She raised her head just a bit and glanced at him through lowered lashes. He wore a hoodie so she still couldn't distinguish his features. She shook her head. "Um, no. I-I haven't seen him."

Her nerves stretched as he continued to stand over her, not acknowledging her response. She started to rise. The stranger's hand snaked around her waist and swept her off her feet. His hand over her mouth cut off her scream. She struggled to no avail, was hustled to the vehicle nearby and shoved to the backseat. The door slammed behind her and her forehead slapped against a hard, male thigh.

The breath whooshed from her as she landed on her belly. Without looking up, she knew whose body she'd landed against. Dominic. His scent—his presence—was unmistakable.

His fingers brushed through her hair and she drew in a sharp breath.

"Don't kill me," she blurted.

Dominic's big hand stilled. "Kill you?" he echoed.

His voice affected her to her core, part fear, part fascination.

"I would never harm you."

He already had. His words had crushed her and—

"You sent Albert." She couldn't keep the anger and accusation out of her voice. She expected more from Dominic, somehow placing him above the antics of Blaine and Garth. "I'll never forget the feel of that barrel pressed to my head." In her side, the press of the gun had frightened her. She knew it could be deadly if he pulled the trigger. But the close contact wound of a head shot left her little to no chance of survival. "You wanted me dead."

Dominic pulled her onto his lap and kissed the top of her head. "Never, Olivia."

Afraid to trust his words, Liv held herself stiff, not wanting to feel so safe and protected in his arms. Not wanting to feel so hurt and alone at the thought of his betrayal. "Just let me go."

"I'll let you go. I'll take you with me. I'll do whatever you ask of me as long as you forgive me. Howie brought Albert to me," he explained, unaware of the hope blooming in Liv's chest.

Hope for a relationship with him. Hope for a future.

"Blaine has him until the authorities—"

"Blaine?" Liv repeated, frowning. Blaine was the last person she wanted to deal with right now.

"Yes. Blaine."

Dominic caressed her back, his touch sending shivers through her. He sighed, nuzzling her neck.

Liv clutched Dominic's forearms, turning her head and covering his mouth with hers. She reveled in the feel of his tongue slipping past her lips and tasting her.

"We can't do this," she whispered after a moment. "You and I can't—"

"Olivia," he murmured, nipping her lips. "I would never trust Blaine with Albert if I thought he'd betray me or try to harm you for the simple fact that he values his freedom more than he values whatever request for help Albert might ask of him."

She sat up and removed herself from temptation by getting off his lap and sitting on the seat. "My brother has no redeeming qualities."

"Do I?"

She sidled a glance at him, unsure. "Do you?"

"I would say very much so. I consider myself a very fair man. I may be a little biased, of course."

Olivia giggled at his wry tone. "You think?"

He chuckled but the sound died away just as fast. Olivia glimpsed Dominic's intensity, his sorrow and regret.

"Forgive me. If you'll give me a chance, I'll make everything up to you. We can start over. Have a try at a real relationship. If that's what you want."

"At the moment I don't really know what I want," she admitted. So much had happened in so short a time.

"I won't rush you, but give me a chance."

He wanted a chance. A chance to be with her and for them to have a future. She really cared about Dominic and wanted to know where their relationship could go, but she'd also seen what happened when love failed. "Thank you for not rushing me. Right now, I want to be alone."

Dominic drew in an agitated breath. "I understand," he gritted out, though he looked anything but understanding. "You must allow me to bring you home. You can't be out here so early in the morning and all alone. It's too dangerous."

Home? Where Blaine is? It dawned on her that she had no home.

Looking out the car window, Liv perused her surroundings. Strategically placed street lights penetrated pockets of pitch black. Until then, she hadn't focused on how eerie and spooky the area was. So quiet. *Now what?*

She certainly couldn't remain here and she refused to return to either Blaine's or Dominic's mansions. Once again, she remembered her no regrets and no running mantra. While it wasn't good to run away, Olivia was beginning to understand her mother's regrets. Had she acted upon them sooner, Connie would've changed her lifestyle.

There it is. Everything in life served a purpose. Even regret. She'd learn from her mistakes as well as her mother's, and would not make the same decisions again. For instance, if she'd told Blaine to go and fuck himself, she *would've* found a job and gotten a roommate, which meant she wouldn't be homeless now.

"Olivia!" Dominic's stern voice pulled her back to the moment.

"You don't have to yell, Dominic," she grouched.

"Apparently, I do. It got your attention." He grabbed her hand and kissed it. "Come along, sweetheart. Let me get you home."

Dominic paused at Olivia's squeak, staring at the fear and confusion settling in her features. It dawned on him where "home" for her was. No fucking way was she ever going back to Bradford.

Her defeated look tore at Dominic's heartstrings. He gathered her in his arms. "It's all right. I'll take you home with me. Until we can secure a place for you," he quickly added when she attempted to push herself out of his arms.

"No, I'm not living with you yet."

He lifted a brow at that. "You've already been living with me."

"Three days?" she scoffed. "Three days of sex and thoughts of retaliation against my brother."

"That's more than any other woman has ever gotten from me romantically."

The moment the words left his mouth, he winced, but Olivia stared at him and burst at laughing. "Your style of romance needs a little work."

Unable to argue, Dominic smiled.

"I want us to have a real relationship," she continued, serious again. "One not guided by lust. If I go with you tonight, it'll turn into a sex fest. Fuck fest...whatever..." She shook her head in frustration.

"Would either one be so bad?"

"No, but life goes on after sex," she said quietly. "It's the after that I want to add to us."

He wanted to add an after-sex to them, too. For so long he'd been focused on how his father had taught him to run the business, that he hadn't realized he'd begun to act like his parents in all areas of his life. With control and manipulation. He wanted more in his life. With Olivia, he had a chance at happiness. No matter what she went through, she kept a positive outlook on life.

He tightened his arms around her. "I understand. I want that too, but you can't live on the street. How about a hotel room tonight and we see about an apartment for you tomorrow?"

She still frowned.

"Olivia," Dominic said with a sigh, holding on to his patience by a thread, "I won't stay in your hotel room. I'll deposit you and leave you to do whatever it is you do."

"The same with the apartment that I don't have money to rent?" she chirped, giving him a cheeky, under-eyed look.

"I can't wait until we're married, Olivia," he blurted. "You're such a source of amusement."

"Your assumption that I'll marry you is laughable!"

Hold on. Did I really say that? Marriage was a long way off. If ever. He couldn't believe he'd thrown those words out there and worked to cover his faux pas.

"I know you don't want to be indebted to anyone so I'll leave it up to you when or how you'll repay me."

She cocked her head to the side. "You know how my mother survived, right?"

"Yes, and I wasn't implying—"

"I won't repay you with sex," she interrupted. "I intend to get a part-time job with hours that'll afford time for my classes."

"I admire your spunk and determination but life itself is expensive. Utilities. Food. Rent."

"I already know what hard work is and what it takes to survive. Only this time, morals win out. Everything I do from here on out will be on the right side of the law."

Dominic nodded in agreement. "C'mon, sweetheart. Let's get you to a hotel."

"As soon as I get my apartment, I want to get my belongings from Blaine's house."

Dominic squeezed her hand. "If that's what you want, that can easily be arranged."

EPILOGUE

Three years later....

Liv adjusted her bridal veil and leaned back in the limousine, smiling. To her, the road to her wedding to Dominic had been long and hard but worth every day of that time.

On that long ago day when she'd retrieved her belongings from Blaine, her brother had gone from shock to contrition in a heartbeat. She suspected his sudden change had been due to Dominic's interest in her and she'd given Blaine the same terms she'd offered Dominic. Give her time. If time proved he was sincere, maybe he could be trusted and they could have a brother-sister relationship.

Happily, he'd done an about-face. They were each other's only living relatives and he'd exhibited real emotion toward her. Like love. He'd also gone overboard to pay for her wedding to Dominic as well as the over-the-top reception that most of the elite hypocrites were invited to.

Thanks to Dominic and his willingness to renegotiate the business deal he'd had with Blaine once he was convinced of her brother's sincerity, Blaine was now one of the top businessmen in the state.

Liv glanced through the limo window as the driver entered the French Quarter, enroute to the St. Louis Cathedral, where she'd soon become Mrs. Dominic Antonio Luca. She sighed dreamily.

She loved him so. Since meeting him, he was always there for her, in all her trials and triumphs. Dominic was her lover, her friend, an almost-husband and a soon-to-be father. She caressed her belly.

Because she'd just recently discovered she was expecting, she hadn't told Dominic yet. They'd planned on kids once she graduated but she'd gone with him on a weekend business trip and had forgotten her pills. She hadn't been overly concerned. When they'd first met and she realized she didn't have the birth control with her, she'd had unprotected sex with him and she hadn't conceived. This time, she had, and this new turn of events overjoyed her.

The limousine pulled to a stop in front of the historic church. Amid gapes, claps and cheers from curious tourists, Olivia was whisked to the vestibule and into an adjoining room, where she waited for her cue to be escorted down the aisle by her brother.

A few hours later, as they lay entwined in each other's arms, Liv decided now would be the perfect time to tell Dominic her news. First, however, she basked in his happiness.

"My Olivia, you don't know how happy you've made me. You're finally mine. All mine," he declared, almost reverently as she lay in his arms.

Well-sated from their lovemaking, she snuggled closer. "Would you like to be even happier?"

"I can't imagine anything else that could add to my joy," he responded and kissed her tenderly.

"How about this? If I have a boy, we can call him Anto. Isn't that short for Antonio? For a girl, Toni might work."

Dominic sat up and brought her with him. The worshipping look on his face brought tears to Olivia's eyes.

"Y-you're giving me a child?" he whispered.

"Would you like a son?"

"It doesn't matter as long as you're its mother."

Too overcome to respond, Olivia wrapped her arms around her husband. She believed she'd made all the right choices at last. She'd won Dominic's heart and his true love. Now, she carried his baby.

She pressed closer to Dominic and he tightened his hold on her. Olivia knew they'd never let each other go.

A Note from Kat

Thank you for reading **Captivated**.
If you enjoyed it, please consider leaving a review
at your point of purchase and on Goodreads. It
means a lot to me to hear what you think.

Books by Kathryn C. Kelly

Phoenix Rising Rock Band Series

Inferno
Incendiary
Inflame

Death Dwellers MC Series

Misled
Misappropriate
Misunderstood
Misdeeds
Misbehavior
Misjudged
Misguided
Misalliance
Misconduct
A Very Christopher Christmas
Misfit
Mistrust
Misgivings
Outlaw's Dictionary
Death Dwellers: The Complete Series

An Outlaw Valentine

Dirty Boys Studio Series

Dirty Boy

Other Titles

All My Tomorrows
Dangerous
Riveted

Pink: Hot 'N Sexy for a cure: The
Books for Boobies 2015 Anthology

Kathryn C. Kelly

When Clubs Collide
Desire Me

WEBSITE: HTTPS://WWW.KATKELWRITER.COM
EMAIL: katkelwriter@outlook.com

About Kathryn C. Kelly

In her dreams, Kathryn Kelly is a flirtatious biker babe with the rumble of a hog between her legs and a shirtless bad boy wrapped in her arms. Kathryn and her bad ass biker boy spend their evenings tossing back great scotch (Chivas Regal) and fighting over who is better at Cards against Humanity (she is, obviously.)

In her reality, Kathryn is a native New Orleanian who has survived Hurricane Katrina and breast cancer. Now she's hoping to survive three lively girls. While not playing Wonder Mom, Kathryn can be found putting all those dreams into the pages of her next Death Dwellers Motorcycle Club novel.

www.ingramcontent.com/pod-product-compliance
Lightning Source LLC
Chambersburg PA
CBHW071119100726
47908CB00008B/2427